The Mysterious Three

William Le Queux

Alpha Editions

This edition published in 2024

ISBN : 9789361471148

Design and Setting By
Alpha Editions
www.alphaedis.com
Email - info@alphaedis.com

As per information held with us this book is in Public Domain.
This book is a reproduction of an important historical work. Alpha Editions uses the best technology to reproduce historical work in the same manner it was first published to preserve its original nature. Any marks or number seen are left intentionally to preserve its true form.

Contents

Chapter One. .... - 1 -
Chapter Two .... - 8 -
Chapter Three. .... - 13 -
Chapter Four. .... - 19 -
Chapter Five. .... - 25 -
Chapter Six. .... - 31 -
Chapter Seven. .... - 38 -
Chapter Eight. .... - 42 -
Chapter Nine. .... - 48 -
Chapter Ten. .... - 53 -
Chapter Eleven. .... - 57 -
Chapter Twelve. .... - 62 -
Chapter Thirteen. .... - 67 -
Chapter Fourteen. .... - 74 -
Chapter Fifteen. .... - 80 -
Chapter Sixteen. .... - 84 -
Chapter Seventeen. .... - 90 -
Chapter Eighteen. .... - 96 -
Chapter Nineteen. .... - 102 -
Chapter Twenty .... - 107 -
Chapter Twenty One. .... - 113 -
Chapter Twenty Two. .... - 118 -
Chapter Twenty Three. .... - 122 -
Chapter Twenty Four. .... - 128 -
Chapter Twenty Five. .... - 135 -
Chapter Twenty Six. .... - 139 -

Chapter Twenty Seven...- 145 -
Chapter Twenty Eight..- 151 -
Chapter Twenty Nine...- 157 -
Chapter Thirty..- 164 -

Chapter One.

Concerns a Visitor.

"Do you know a Mr Smithson, Gwen?" Sir Charles Thorold asked his wife abruptly as he stood astride before the big fire in the hall.

"Smithson?" Lady Thorold answered as she poured out the tea. "No. Who is he?"

"I have no idea. Never heard of him."

Then, addressing the butler, Sir Charles asked anxiously—

"Did he leave a card, James?"

"No, Sir Charles. He asked to see you—or her ladyship."

"Or me?" Lady Thorold exclaimed. "Why, how very mysterious. What was he like?"

"A tall, powerfully-built man, m'lady."

"A gentleman?"

"M'yes, m'lady. He came in a car."

As James said this in his grave, solemn way, I saw Vera Thorold's eyes twinkle with amusement. For Sir Charles's only child possessed that gift rare in a woman—a sense of humour.

"You are sure you have the name right?" Thorold said, after a moment's pause.

"Quite, Sir Charles. I think he was not going to give his name, as you were out. I asked him what name, and he seemed to hesitate, then he said: 'Oh, say Mr Smithson called, Sir Charles knows me,' and then he seemed to smile, Sir Charles."

"He seemed to smile. I wonder why?"

His master turned to Lady Thorold.

"What do you make of it, Gwen?"

"I make nothing of it," replied his wife. "Is it some friend of yours, Vera?"

"Mother, how ridiculous," the girl exclaimed; "as if I should have a friend called 'Smithson'!"

"Pardon me, Sir Charles, but—" broke in the butler.

"Well, what?"

"There is a portrait of him in the morning-room."

"A portrait?" gasped his master. "A portrait of Smithson! Then why the deuce didn't you say so before! Which is it? I should really like to know."

"There are so many portraits in the morning-room," Lady Thorold interrupted, "we had better go in, and James will show us which it is. He may have mistaken the name, after all."

We all got up from tea in the hall, made our way to the drawing-room, and thence into the morning-room, which opened out of it. There was plenty of daylight still. James came in after us, and went straight up to a framed panel portrait which stood with others on a small table in a remote corner. It showed a tall handsome, clean-shaved man of three or four and thirty, of fine physique, seated astride a chair, his arms folded across the back of the chair as he faced the camera.

"This is the one, Sir Charles," the butler said, pointing to it.

I distinctly saw Lady Thorold give a start. Sir Charles, tanned though his face was by wind and sun, turned quite pale. Vera, who was standing by me at the moment, suddenly gripped my arm, I think unconsciously. As I glanced down at her I noticed that her eyes were set upon her mother. They had in them an expression of deep anxiety, almost of terror. Sir Charles was the first to recover his composure.

"Oh—that one," he exclaimed slowly, with a forced laugh. "Then there is no mystery at all. His giving the name 'Smithson' was of course his joke. Now we know why he smiled. Thank you, James. You can go."

I confess that I was puzzled. Indeed, I felt greatly mystified, and to some extent perturbed. I knew quite well by my host's tone and manner and by the look in Lady Thorold's eyes, perhaps most of all by that squeeze Vera had unconsciously given my arm, that all three had received some very unpleasant, apparently some terrible shock. But why? And what could have caused it? Who was that big man whose portrait stood framed there? What was his name? Why had he called himself "Smithson"? What was the mystery concerning him in relation to my hosts, or the mystery concerning my hosts in relation to him? My curiosity was keenly aroused.

I don't think I am likely ever to forget that date—Wednesday, February 5, 1911, for it marks the beginning of a train of events so remarkable, I would call it amazing only I am not addicted to talking in superlatives. Yet I do assure you that I in no way exaggerate, and that the story I am about to tell is but a record of bare facts.

That February morning was quite bright and balmy, I remember it because it was the first day of the Waterloo Cup meeting. Rather warm, indeed, for hunting, and at the meet and the coverside the scraps of conversation one overheard referred chiefly to a big ball at Oakham.

Hounds had not been thrown into Colly Weston Wood more than a quarter of an hour when a piercing "View Holloa" echoed through the wood, and a long, lean, yellow-bodied fox broke away not two hundred yards from the spot where the majority of the field sat waiting on their impatient, fidgety mounts, and with a single glance behind him at the mottled pack streaming out of the cover in full cry, crossed a ploughed field, popped through a hedge and disappeared.

A few moments later came the usual wild stampede, and in less than a minute hounds and horses were fast disappearing in the distance, the music of the flying pack growing rapidly fainter in the distance.

By a singular stroke of ill-luck—or so I thought it then—I had got left. I had set my horse at a treacherous stake-and-wattle fence, hoping thus to steal a march on the rest of the field galloping wildly for a couple of open gates. My horse had blundered, I daresay partly through my fault, and had staked himself, though only slightly. To cut a long story short, my day's amusement was over, for, after doing what I could to staunch the bleeding, I had to lead the poor beast all the way home to Houghton Park, a distance of at least eight miles.

Naturally I expected to be home long before my host, Sir Charles Thorold, and his wife and daughter, for as I entered the Park gates, with my lame animal crawling slowly after me, it was barely three o'clock. I was a good deal surprised, therefore to see Sir Charles and the two coming along another of the Park roads, and not a hundred yards away from me. They had entered by another gate.

"Hello, Ashton!" Thorold called out to me cheerily. "Why, where have you been, and what is amiss?"

I explained as soon as we were all together, and he sympathised. So did Miss Thorold. She was genuinely sorry I had missed the really splendid run.

"We all missed our second horses," she added, "and our animals were so dead beat that we decided to come home, though hounds were, I believe, going to draw again."

Her sympathy soothed me a good deal, for I think that even then I was in love with the tall, graceful, fair-haired girl who, on horseback, looked so perfectly bewitching. The exercise, the fresh air and the excitement of the morning's sport had combined to give a colour to her cheeks and to impart a singular brightness to her eyes that together enhanced her quite exceptional loveliness.

Though I could remember her as a child, I had not seen her for eleven years until a fortnight previously, her father had invited me to Houghton Park, in Rutland. He had invited me the previous year, but on that occasion Vera had been away in Switzerland.

We had got rid of our muddy hunting kit, indulged in hot baths, and, feeling delightfully clean and comfortable and at peace with all the world, were at tea in the great hall of Houghton, a fine, many-gabled country mansion, with rows of twisted chimneys said to date back to a period of Elizabeth, when James the butler, calm and stately—I can see him still—had walked in his slow, dignified manner into the hall, to tell Sir Charles that "a gentleman had called shortly before he returned," a gentleman named Smithson.

We went back to the big oak-panelled hall to finish our tea, and though Sir Charles and Lady Thorold made light of the incident, and quickly changed the subject of conversation, the entire "atmosphere" seemed somehow different. Our relations appeared suddenly to have become quite strained.

Half an hour later I found Vera in the library. I had noticed that, since our return downstairs, my presence had been distasteful to her—or at least I thought so.

She was seated on a big settee, near the fire, pretending to read a newspaper, but her fingers twitched nervously, and presently I saw one hand squeeze the paper convulsively.

I tossed away my cigarette, and crossed over to her.

"Vera," I said in a low tone, "tell me what is amiss. What has happened? why do you look so worried?"

We were alone, and the door was closed.

She looked up, and her eyes met mine. Her lips parted as if she were about to speak, then they shut tightly. Suddenly she bit her lip, and her big, expressive eyes filled with tears.

"Vera," I said very gently, sinking down beside her, for I felt a strange affinity between us—an affinity of soul, "What is it? What's the matter? Tell me, dear. I won't tell a soul."

I couldn't help it. My arm stole round her waist and my lips touched her cold forehead. Had she sprung away from me, turned upon me with flaming eyes and boxed my ears even, I should have been less surprised than at what happened, for never before had I taken such a liberty. Instead, she turned her pretty head, sank with a sigh upon my shoulder, and an instant later her arms encircled my neck. She was sobbing bitterly, so terribly that I feared she was about to become hysterical.

"Oh, Mr Ashton!" she burst out, "oh, if you only knew!"

"Knew what?" I whispered. "Tell me. I won't breathe it to a single living person."

"But that's it," she exclaimed as she still wept bitterly. "I don't know—but I suspect—I fear something so terribly, and yet I don't know what it is!"

This was an enigma I had not looked for.

"What is going to happen?" I asked, more to say something, anything, than to sit there speechless and supine.

"If only I knew I would tell you," she answered between her sobs, "I would tell you sooner than anybody because—oh, I love you so, I love you so!"

I shall never forget how my heart seemed to spring within me at those blessed words.

"Vera! My darling!"

She was in my arms. I was kissing her passionately. Now I knew what I had not before realised—I was desperately in love with Vera Thorold, this beautiful girl with the wonderful, deep eyes and the glorious hair, who when I had last seen her, had been still a child in short frocks, though lovely then.

Footsteps were approaching. Quickly we sprang apart as the door opened.

"Her ladyship wishes you to come at once, mademoiselle," said a voice in the shadow in what struck me as being rather a disagreeable tone, with a slightly foreign accent. It was Judith, Lady Thorold's French maid.

Vera rose at once. For a brief instant her eyes met mine. Then she was gone.

I sat there in the big book-lined room quite alone, smoking cigarette after cigarette, wondering and wondering. Who was "Smithson?" What was this strange, unexpected mystery? Above all, what was this trouble that Vera dreaded so, or was it merely some whim of her imagination? I knew her to be of a highly-strung, super-sensitive nature.

The big grandfather-clock away in a corner hissed and wheezed for some moments, then slowly struck seven. I waited for the dressing gong to sound. Usually James, or the footman, Henry, appeared as soon as the clock had finished striking, and made an intolerable noise upon the gong. Five minutes passed, ten, fifteen. Evidently the gong had been forgotten, for Sir Charles dined punctually at the unfashionable hour of half-past seven. I rose and went upstairs to dress.

At the half-hour I came down and went towards the small drawing-room where they always assemble before dinner. To my surprise the room was in darkness.

"Something seems to be amiss to-night," I remember saying mentally as I switched on the light. The domestic service at Houghton was habitually like clockwork in its regularity.

A quarter to eight struck. Eight o'clock! I began to wonder if dinner had been put off. A quarter-past eight chimed out.

I went over to the fireplace and pressed the electric bell. Nobody came. I pressed it again. Finally I kept my finger pressed upon it.

This was ridiculous. Thoroughly annoyed, I went into the dining-room. It was in darkness. Then I made my way out to the servants' quarters. James was sitting in the pantry, in his shirt sleeves, smoking a cigar. A brandy bottle stood upon the dresser, and a syphon, also a half-empty tumbler.

"Is anything the matter, James?" I asked, with difficulty concealing the irritation I felt.

"Not as I know of," he answered in rather a rude tone. I saw at once that he had been drinking.

"At what time is dinner?"

"Dinner?"

He laughed outright.

"There ain't no dinner. Why ain't you gone too?"

"Gone? Where?"

"With Sir Charles and her ladyship and Miss Vera and Judith."

"I don't understand you. What do you mean?"

"They went an hour ago, or more."

"Went where?"

"Oh, ask me another. I don't know."

James in his cups was a very different person from sober, respectful, deferential James. And then it came back to me that, about an hour before, I had heard a car going down the avenue, and wondered whose it was.

The sound of loud, coarse laughter reached me from the kitchen.

"Well, all I says is it's a pretty state of things," a woman's high, harsh voice exclaimed. I think it was the cook's. "Cleared and gone with bags and baggage as if the devil hisself was after 'em."

"P'r'aps 'e is," a man's voice, that I recognised as Henry's, announced, and again came peals of laughter.

This was a pleasant situation, certainly. My hosts vanished. The butler drunk. The servants apparently in rebellion!

Restlessly I paced the hall. My thoughts always work quickly, and my mind was soon made up.

First I went to the telephone, rang up the *Stag's Head Hotel* in Oakham, the nearest town—it was eight miles off—and asked the proprietor, whom I knew personally, to send me out a car as quickly as possible, also to reserve a room for me for the night. Then I went into the morning-room, tucked the big panel photograph, in its frame, under my arm, took it up to my room, and deposited it in the bottom of my valise. As I finished packing my clothes and other belongings I heard the car hooting as it came quickly up the long beech avenue leading from the lodge-gates.

My valise was not heavy, and I am pretty strong. Also I am not proud. I lifted it on to my bed, crouched down, hoisted the valise on to my back, as the railway porters do, carried it downstairs, and let the driver have it. He was a man I knew, and I noticed that he was grinning.

"Taking physical exercise, sir?" he asked lightly.

"Yes," I answered, "it's better sport than foxhunting."

He laughed outright, then helped me into my overcoat. A minute later we were on the road to Oakham.

And all the while the sad face of the girl for whom I had that evening declared my love—as I had last seen it, with her eyes set on mine as though in mute appeal—kept rising before me like a vision.

Chapter Two.

Contains Certain Revelations.

Until lunch-time next day I remained in Oakham, not knowing what to do, uncertain what steps to take.

I am a bachelor with a comfortable income, and, I am ashamed to say, an idler. Work never did really appeal to me. I try to compensate for not working by paying my taxes regularly and being as charitable as I can to people I come across and like, and whom the world seems to treat unjustly.

My father, Richard Ashton, was Colonel in the Blues. I was his only child, for my mother died in bringing me into the world to live at ease and waste my time. When my father died I found myself heir to a small property in Rutland, which I promptly let, and One Hundred and Eighty Thousand pounds safely invested—mostly in Consols. Sport in general, especially hunting and shooting, also reading, constitute my favourite forms of recreation. Generally I live in London, where I have a flat in King Street, St. James's.

I don't remember what made me do it, but while lunching at the *Stag's Head* I decided that I would take the car out to Houghton Park again. I think I was curious to see if any fresh development had taken place there.

Nobody answered my repeated rings at the front door, so I went round to the back. The door was locked. I rang, and rang again, and knocked. But nobody came.

I walked right round the house. Every window was shut, and apparently fastened. The whole place was as still as death. Then I went to the stables. I could hear the occasional rattle of a headstall chain, but the horses were all locked in.

Having lit a cigar and told my driver to await my return, I sauntered aimlessly up into the woods—Houghton Park is one of the most beautifully wooded estates in Rutland, with a lake seven acres in extent hidden away in a delightfully picturesque spot surrounded by pine-grown hills. Several times during the past fortnight I had rambled up into these woods accompanied by Vera, and the association brought her back into my thoughts with renewed vividness. Where was she at that moment? What was she doing? Was she happy? Had any evil befallen her? When should I hear of her again? When should I see her?

These, and many other reflections, came crowding in confusion into my brain. What could be the meaning of this extraordinary mystery, so suddenly created, so unexpected? I had known Sir Charles and Lady Thorold many years, in fact since I was a child. For years they had lived in London—in Belgravia. Then, two years previously, they had rented Houghton Park and come to live there. The "County people" of Rutland are perhaps as conservative as any in England, and, knowing little about Sir Charles and Lady Thorold, who had received their title through political influence before settling in that county, they had not made haste to call.

As soon, however, as it had become known that the new arrivals were extremely rich, also that Sir Charles meant to entertain largely, and was going to hunt, and that the Houghton covers were to be well preserved, the barriers of exclusiveness upon which the old families so pride themselves, had been quickly swept away.

Somewhat out of breath after my slow climb up through the woods, I rested at the top of the hill, from which a glorious view could be obtained of the picturesque landscape of early spring, that unfolded itself as far as sight could reach, a perfect panorama of our beautiful English scenery that Americans so much admire, probably because it affords so striking a contrast to their never-ending prairies and gigantic mountains. Upon the opposite side of the hill on which I stood, deep down in a ravine thick with brambles and undergrowth, the face of the placid lake glistened like a mirror between the budding trees, sparkling here and there with a blinding brightness where the sun shone straight upon it.

A pheasant springing into the air within a yard of me made me jump, and brought my wandering thoughts quickly back to earth. Why had I rambled up here? I could not say. I had walked and climbed in a kind of dream, so deeply was my mind engrossed with thoughts of what had happened and with conjectures as to the future. And now, unconsciously, my attention gradually became centred upon the lake, or rather upon a curious-looking, dark object among the weeds upon its surface, within a stone's throw of the bank.

I glanced at my watch. It was barely three o'clock. I had nothing at all to do, so decided to make my way down through the undergrowth and find out what this strange object might be.

Yes, I had not been mistaken. The first impression I had formed had been the right one, though I had tried to persuade myself it could not be. I was standing on the bank now, not ten yards from the object, and I could see distinctly what it was. A human body, fully clothed, lay there motionless—a man's body, face downward, the head almost submerged.

My first thought was to plunge in and swim out to it and try to rescue the drowning man. But an instant's reflection caused me to refrain. The man, whoever he was, must be dead. He had been there a long time, or the head would not have sunk, nor, indeed, would the body have floated.

I made my way as quickly as I could along the footpath on the bank until I reached the boathouse, a hundred yards away. It was locked. With a big stone I shattered the padlock, and in a minute I was rowing towards the body.

With some difficulty I succeeded in hitching the painter round the feet. Having at last done so, I rowed back to the bank, towing the drowned man.

And there I turned the body over. It must have been in the water many hours, probably all night, I saw at once. And directly I saw the face I recognised it, drawn and disfigured though it was.

The drowned man was Thorold's butler, James.

What had happened? Had he fallen into the lake while under the influence of drink? Had he committed suicide? Or had he—

Somehow this last reflection startled me. Was it possible there had been foul play?

I had to leave the body there, for I found it impossible to lift it on to the bank without help.

"The great house," as the tenantry called it, was still locked when I got back there. Silence still reigned everywhere. The driver of my taxi was fast asleep on his seat.

When I prodded him with my stick he sat up with a start, and apologised.

"Get back to Oakham as quickly as you can," I said to him as I stepped into the car and slammed the door.

He turned his starting handle without result. He lifted the bonnet, and for a long time examined the machinery. Then, removing his coat, he wormed himself underneath the car, lying flat upon his back.

When at last he emerged he was red in the face and perspiring freely.

"Oh, by the way, sir," he said suddenly, picking up his coat and thrusting his hand into one of its pockets, "I think you dropped this."

As he stopped speaking he pulled his hand out and held out to me a little silver flask about four inches square.

I took it, and examined it.

"This isn't mine," I said. "Where did you find it?"

"Just there, sir," and he pointed to the ground beside the car.

When I looked at the flask again, I noticed that the tiny shield in the middle was engraved. The engraving was a cipher, which, on scrutinising closely, I made out to be the letters "D.P." intertwined.

I unscrewed the stopper and smelt the contents. The smell, though peculiar, was not wholly unfamiliar. Still, for the moment I could not classify it.

"Didn't you drop it, sir?"

"No."

"Then perhaps I had better take it," and he held out his hand.

"No, I'll keep it—you needn't be anxious," I said. "I have been staying here, and probably it belongs to somebody in the house, or to somebody who has called."

I fumbled in my pocket and produced two half-crowns, which at once allayed any conscientious squeamishness afflicting the driver at the thought of handing over his treasure-trove to a stranger.

But where was Vera? Where, indeed, were the Thorolds?

The chauffeur continued to overhaul his engine and its complicated mechanism. While he was thus engaged I poured a little of the fluid out of the flask, which was quite full. The colour was a dark, transparent brown, almost the shade of old brandy. Somehow I could not help thinking that this flask might—

And yet, why should it prove a clue? What reason was there to suppose it had been dropped by the strange visitor on the previous day, the mysterious Smithson?

"Hullo, sir, this is curious!"

My driver was bending over the machinery he had been examining so closely. His hands, which had previously been in the gear-box resembled a nigger's, only they looked more slimy.

"What is it?" I asked, approaching him.

"The plugs have been tampered with. No wonder she wouldn't start. Look."

He was holding out a damaged sparking-plug.

I own a car and, being well acquainted with its intricacies, saw at once that what he said was true. Somebody—presumably while he was wandering about the lawns and back premises—must have lifted the bonnet and injured the plugs. There was no other solution. The car could not have travelled out from Oakham, or travelled at all, had that damage been done before.

We looked at each other, equally puzzled.

"You ain't been playing me a trick, sir?" he said suddenly, an expression of mistrust coming into his eyes.

"Oh, don't be a fool!" I answered irritably.

He turned sulky.

"Some one 'as, anyway," he grunted. "And it's just a chance I've some spare plugs with me."

He produced his tool-box, rummaged among its contents with his filthy hands, discovered what he wanted, and adjusted them. Then he shut down the bonnet with a vicious bang and set his engine going.

He was about to step on to his seat, when simultaneously a sharp report a good way off and the "zip" of a bullet close to us made us spring away in alarm.

Together, without uttering a word, we gazed up towards the wood on the hill, where the sound of the report had come from.

Another shot rang out. This time the bullet shattered the car headlight.

"Ah! God!" the driver gasped. "Help! I—I—"

Poor fellow. Those were his last words. Almost as he uttered them there came a third report, and the driver, shot through the head, collapsed into a heap beside the car.

And then, what I saw as I turned sharply, sent a shiver through me.

I held my breath. What further mystery was there?

Surely some great evil had fallen upon the house of the Thorolds.

Chapter Three.

The Name of "Smithson."

A man was kneeling, facing me, on the outskirts of the wood on the hill, not a hundred yards away. His face was in shadow, and partly hidden by a slouch hat, so that I could hardly see it. The rifle he held was levelled at me—he was taking steady aim—his left arm extended far up the barrel, so that his hand came near the muzzle—the style adopted by all first-class shots, as it ensures deadly accuracy.

I am bound to confess that I completely lost my nerve. I sprang to one side almost as he fired. I had just enough presence of mind left to pick up the driver in my arms—even at the risk of my life I couldn't leave him there—lift him into the car, and slam the door. Then I jumped on to the driving-seat, put in the clutch—in a perfect frenzy of fear lest I myself should be shot at the next instant—and the car flew down the avenue.

Twice I heard reports, and with the second one came the sound of a whistling bullet. But it went wide of the mark.

The lodge came quickly into view. It was well out of sight of the wood on the hill where the shots had been fired. I uttered an exclamation as I saw that the big white gate was shut. It was hardly ever shut.

Slowing down, I brought the car to a standstill within a few yards of the lodge, jumped out, and ran forward to open the gate.

It was fastened with a heavy chain, and the chain was securely padlocked.

Shouting failed to bring any one out of the lodge, so I clambered over the gate and knocked loudly at the door. But nobody answered, and, when I tried to open the door, I found it locked.

There seemed to be but one way out of the difficulty. I have said that I am strong, yet it needed all my strength to lift that heavy gate off its hinges. It fell with a crash back into the road, and I managed to drag it away to one side. Then starting the engine again, I set off once more for Oakham "all out."

I went straight to the hospital, but a brief examination of the poor fellow sufficed to assure the doctors that the man was already dead. Then I went to the police-station and told them everything I knew—how a man giving the name "Smithson" had called at Houghton Park to see Sir Charles Thorold; how Thorold had repudiated all knowledge of the man; how Sir Charles and Lady Thorold and their daughter, and Lady Thorold's maid, Judith—I did not know her surname—had suddenly left Houghton, and mysteriously disappeared; how I had, that afternoon, found the house shut up, though I had seen a man disappear from one of the windows; how I had discovered the butler's body in the lake; how my driver had been shot dead by some one hidden in a wood upon a hill, and how other shots had been fired at me by the assassin.

At first the police seemed inclined to detain me, but when I had convinced them that I was what they quaintly termed "a bona fide gentleman," and had produced what they called my "credentials,"—these consisted of a visiting card, and of a letter addressed to me at Houghton Park—and given them my London address and telephone number, they let me go. I found out afterwards that, while they kept me talking at the station, they had telephoned to London, in order to verify my statements that I had a flat in King Street and belonged to Brooks's Club.

The coffee room of the *Stag's Head Hotel* that night was crowded, for it was the night of the Hunt Ball, and every available bed in the hotel had been engaged some days in advance. Those dining were all strangers to me, most of them young people in very high spirits.

"I've kept this table for you, sir," the head waiter said, as he conducted me across the room. "It is the best I could do; the other place at it is engaged."

"And by a beautiful lady, I hope," I answered lightly, for I knew this waiter to be something of a wag.

"No, sir," he answered with a grin, "by a gentleman with a beard. A charming gentleman, sir. You'll like him."

"Who is he? What is he like?"

"Oh, quite a little man, sir, with a nervous, fidgetty manner, and a falsetto voice. Ah," he added, lowering his voice, "here he comes."

There was a twinkle of merriment in the waiter's eyes, as he turned and hurried away to meet the giant who had just entered the room. I don't think I had ever before seen so tall and magnificent-looking a man. He must have stood quite six feet four, and was splendidly built. His dark, deep-set eyes peered out with singular power from beneath bushy brows. He had a high, broad forehead, and thick black hair. His beard, well-trimmed, reached just below his white tie, for of course he was in evening clothes.

There was a noticeable lull in the buzz of conversation as the newcomer appeared, and all eyes were set upon him as he strolled with an easy, swinging gait across the room towards my table. I saw dowagers raise their lorgnettes and scrutinise him with great curiosity, mingled with approval, as he went along.

Instinctively I rose as he approached. I don't know why I did. I should not have risen had any ordinary stranger been brought over to my table to occupy a vacant seat. The man looked down at me, smiled—it was a most friendly, captivating smile—nodded genially, and then seated himself facing me. I am a bit of a snob at heart—most of us are, only we won't admit it—and I felt gratified at the reflected interest I knew was now being taken in me, for many people were staring hard at us both, evidently thinking that this remarkable-looking stranger must be Somebody, and that, as we were apparently acquainted, I must be Somebody too.

The waiter's eye caught mine, and I heard him give a low chuckle of satisfaction at the practical joke he had played upon me.

"I suppose you are also going to the ball, sir," the big man said to me in his great, deep voice, when he had told the waiter what to bring him.

"No, I'm not. I rather wish I were," I answered. "Unfortunately, however, I have to return to town to-night. Are you going?"

"To town?"

"No, to the ball."

He hesitated before answering.

"Yes—well, perhaps," he said, as he began his soup. "I am not yet certain. I want to go, but there are reasons why I should not," and he smiled.

"That sounds rather curious."

"It is very curious, but it is so."

"Do you mind explaining?"

"I do."

His eyes were set on mine. They seemed somehow to hold my gaze in fascination. There was in them an expression that was half ironical, half humorous.

"I believe this is the first time we have met," he said, after a pause.

"I'm quite sure it is," I answered. "You will forgive my saying so, but I don't think any one who had once met you could very well forget it."

He gave a great laugh.

"Perhaps you are right—ah! perhaps you are right," he said laughing, wiping his moustache and mouth with his napkin. "Certainly I shall never forget you."

I began, for the first time, to feel rather uncomfortable. He seemed to talk in enigmas. He was evidently what I believe is called "a character."

"Do you know this part of the country well?" I asked, anxious to change the subject.

"Yes—and no," he answered slowly, thoughtfully.

This was getting tiresome. I began to think he was trying to make fun of me. I began to wish the waiter had not put him to sit at my table.

Presently he looked again across at me, and said quite suddenly—

"Look here, Mr Ashton, let us understand each other at once, shall we?"

His eyes looked into mine again, and I again felt quite uneasy. He knew my name. I felt distinctly annoyed at the waiter having told him my name without first asking my permission, as I concluded he must have done. It was a great liberty on his part, I considered—an impertinence, more especially as he had not mentioned this stranger's name to me.

"I shall not be at the ball—and yet I shall be there," the big man continued, as I did not speak. "Tell me, do you return to Houghton after going to London?"

"You seem to know a good deal about me, Mr —" I said, rather nettled, but hoping to draw his name from him.

He did not take the hint.

"Sir Charles is well, I hope? And Lady Thorold?" he went on. "And how is their charming daughter, Miss Vera? I have not seen her for some days. She seems to be as fond as ever of hunting. I think it a cold-blooded, brutal sport. In fact I don't call it 'sport' at all—twenty or so couples of hounds after one fox, and the chances all in favour of the hounds. I have told her so more than once, and I believe that in her heart she agrees with me. As a matter of fact, I'm here in Oakham, on purpose to call on Sir Charles to-morrow, on a matter of business."

I was astounded, also annoyed. Who on earth was this big man, who seemed to know so much, who spoke of Vera as though he knew her intimately and met her every day, and who apparently was acquainted also with Sir Charles and Lady Thorold, yet whom I had never before set eyes on, though I was so very friendly with the Thorolds?

The stranger had spoken of my well-beloved!

"You will forgive my asking you, I am sure," I said, curiosity getting the better of me, "but—well, I have not the pleasure of knowing your name. Do you mind telling me?"

"Mind telling you my name?" he exclaimed, with a look of surprise. "Why, not in the least. My name is—well—Smithson—if you like. Any name will do?"

He must have noticed my sudden change of expression, for he said at once—

"You seem surprised?"

"I—well, I am rather surprised. But you merely are not Smithson," I answered awkwardly. I was staring hard at him, scrutinising his face in order to discover some resemblance to the portrait which at that moment lay snugly at the bottom of my valise. The portrait showed a clean-shaven man, younger than this strange individual whom I had met, as I believed, for the first time, barely a quarter of an hour before. Age might have wrought changes, and the beard might have served as a disguise, but the man in the picture was certainly over thirty-four, and my companion here at dinner could not have been less than forty-five at most. Even the eyes, those betrayers of disguised faces, bore no resemblance that I could see to the eyes of the man in the picture. The beard and moustache of the man facing me were certainly not artificial. That I could see at a glance.

"Why are you surprised?" the man asked abruptly.

"It would take a long time to explain," I answered, equivocating, "but it is a curious coincidence that only yesterday I almost met a man named Smithson. I was wondering if he could be some relation of yours. He was not like you in face."

"Oh, so you know Smithson?"

"No, I don't know him. I have never met him. I said I *almost* met him."

"Have you never seen him, then?"

"Never in my life."

"And yet you say he is 'not like me in face.' How do you know he is not like me in face if you have never seen him?"

The sudden directness of his tone disconcerted me. For an instant I felt like a witness being cross-examined by a bullying Counsel.

"I've seen a portrait of him."

"Indeed?"

My companion raised his eyebrows.

"And where did you see a portrait of him?" he inquired pointedly.

This was embarrassing. Why was he suddenly so interested, so inquisitive? I had no wish to make statements which I felt might lead to my being dragged into saying all sorts of things I had no wish to say, especially to a stranger who, though he had led me to believe that he was acquainted with the Thorolds, apparently had no inkling of what had just happened at Houghton Park.

No inkling! I almost smiled as the thought occurred to me, and was quickly followed by the thought of the sensation the affair would create when the newspapers came to hear of what had happened, and began to "spread themselves" upon the subject, as they certainly would do very soon.

My companion's voice dispelled my wandering reflections.

"Where did you see the portrait of this other Smithson?" he asked, looking at me oddly.

"In a friend's house."

"Was it at Houghton Park?"

"In point of fact, it was."

His eyes seemed to read my thoughts, and I didn't like it. He was silent for some moments. Then suddenly he rose.

"Well, Mr Ashton," he said quite genially, as he extended his hand, "I am glad that we have met, and I trust we shall meet again. 'In point of fact,' to use your own phrase, we shall, and very soon. Until then—good-bye. I have enjoyed our little conversation. It has been so—what shall I say—informal, and it was so unexpected. I did not expect to meet you to-night, I can assure you."

He was gone, leaving me in a not wholly pleasant frame of mind. The man puzzled me. Did I like him, or did I not? His personality attracted me, had done so from the moment I had set eyes on him framed in the doorway, but I was bound to admit that some of his observations had annoyed me. In particular, that remark: "We shall meet again, and very soon;" also his last words: "I did not expect to meet you to-night, I can assure you," caused me some uneasiness in the face of all that had happened. Indeed all through dinner his remarks had somehow seemed to bear some hidden meaning.

Chapter Four.

Further Mystery.

I had to go up to London that night. My lawyers had written some days previously that they must see me personally at the earliest possible moment on some matter to do with my investments, which they controlled entirely, and the letter had been left lying at my flat in King Street before being forwarded. And as the Oakham police had impressed upon me that my presence would be needed in Oakham within the next day or two, I had decided to run up to London, see my lawyers and get my interview with them over, and then return to Rutland as soon as possible.

Again and again, as the night express tore through the darkness towards St. Pancras, Vera's fair face and appealing eyes floated like a vision into my thoughts. I must see her again, at once—but how could I find her, and where? Would the police try to find her, and her father and mother? But why should they? After all, perhaps Sir Charles and Lady Thorold's flight from Houghton did not mean that they intended to conceal themselves. What reason could they have for concealment?

Then, all at once, an idea occurred to me. I smiled at my stupidity in not thinking of it before. There was the Thorolds' house in Belgrave Street. It had been shut up for a long time, but perhaps for some reason they had suddenly decided to go back there. On my arrival at St. Pancras I would at once ring up that house and inquire if they were there.

But I was doomed to disappointment. While the porter was hailing a taxi for me, I went to the station telephone. There were plenty of Thorolds in the telephone-directory that hung inside the glass door, but Sir Charles' name was missing.

Determined not to be put off, I told the driver to go first to Belgrave Street. The number of the Thorolds' house was, I remembered, a hundred and two. By the time we got there it was past midnight. The house bore no sign of being occupied. I was about to ring, when a friendly constable with a bull's-eye lantern prevented me.

"It's empty, sir," he said; "has been for months and months, in fact as long as I can remember."

"But surely there is a caretaker," I exclaimed.

"Oh, there's a caretaker, a very old man," he answered with a grin. "But you won't get *him* to come down at this time of night. He's a character, he is."

There had been nothing in the newspapers that day, but, on the morning after, the bomb burst.

AMAZING STORY
WELL-KNOWN FAMILY VANISH
BUTLER'S BODY IN THE LAKE

Those headlines, in what news-editors call "war type," met my eyes as I unfolded the paper.

I was in bed, and my breakfast on the tray beside me grew cold while I devoured the three columns of close-set print describing everything that had occurred from the moment of Sir Charles' disappearance until the paper had gone to press.

I caught my breath as I came to my own name. My appearance was described in detail, names of my relatives were given, and a brief outline of my father's brilliant career—for he had been a great soldier—and then all my movements during the past two days were summarised.

I had last been seen, the account ran, dining at the *Stag's Head Hotel* with a gentleman, a stranger, whom nobody seemed to know anything about. He had come to the *Stag's Head* on the evening of Monday, April 1, engaged a bedroom and a sitting-room in the name of Davies, and he had left on the night of Wednesday, April 3. He had intended, according to the newspaper, to sleep at the *Stag's Head* that night, but between ten and eleven o'clock he had changed his mind, packed his suit-case, paid his bill, and left. Where he had come from, none knew; where he had gone, or why, none knew. How he had spent his time from his arrival until his departure, nobody had been able to discover.

"All that is known about him," ran the newspaper report, "is that he was a personal friend of Mr Richard Ashton, and that he dined at the *Stag's Head Hotel* with Mr Ashton on the Wednesday evening, his last meal in the hotel before his hurried departure."

This was horrible. It seemed to convey indirectly the impression that I knew why the Thorolds had disappeared, and where they had gone. More, a casual reader might easily have been led to suppose that I was implicated in some dark plot, involving the death of the butler. I appeared in the light of a man of mystery, the friend of a man who might, for aught I knew, be some criminal, but whose name—this certainly interested me—he apparently intended should remain secret.

I turned over the page. Good heavens—my portrait! And the one portrait of myself that of all others I detested. Anybody looking at that particular portrait would at once say: "What a villainous man; he looks like a criminal!"

I remembered now, rather bitterly, making that very observation when the proofs had been sent to me by the photographer, and how my friends had laughed and said it was "quite true," and that it resembled a portrait in a Sunday paper of "the accused in Court."

There were also portraits of Sir Charles and Lady Thorold, and a pretty picture of Vera, the best that had ever been taken of her. But the one portrait that I felt ought to have been reproduced, though it was not, was one of the bearded giant, who had given his name as Davies.

Thoroughly disgusted, I turned without appetite to my tepid breakfast. I had hardly begun to eat, when the telephone at my bedside rang.

Was that Mr Richard Ashton's flat? asked a voice. Might the speaker speak to him?

Mr Ashton was speaking.

"Oh, this was the office of *The Morning*. The editor would greatly appreciate Mr Ashton's courtesy if he would receive one of his representatives. He would not detain him long."

I gulped a mouthful of tea, then explained that I would sooner not be interviewed. I was extremely sorry, I said, that my name had been dragged into this extraordinary affair.

The news-editor was persistent. I was firm. I always am firm when I am at the end of a telephone, but rarely on other occasions. Finally I rang off.

A brief interval. Then another ring. Well, what?

"The editor of the—"

"No," I answered as politely as I could. "I am extremely sorry. You see, I have just refused to be interviewed by *The Morning*, and it would hardly be fair to that journal if... Oh, *The Morning* was a paper of no consequence, was it? That made a difference, of course, but still... no... no... I was really sorry... I could not... I..."

I hung up the receiver. As I did so my man entered. There were four gentlemen downstairs, also a photographer. They wanted to know if—

"Tell them," I interrupted, "that I cannot see them. And, John—"

"Sir?"

"I am not at home to anybody—anybody at all. You understand?"

"Quite, sir."

I noticed that his tone was not quite as deferential as usual. I knew the reason. Of course he had seen this odious paper, or some paper more odious still.

Probably he and the other servants in the building had been discussing me, and hazarding all sorts of wildly improbable stories about me.

The telephone bell rang again. I forget what I said. I think it was a short prayer, or an invocation of some kind. My first impulse was not to answer the 'phone again at all, but to let the thing go on ringing. It rang so persistently, however, that in desperation I pulled off the receiver.

"Who the dickens is it? What do you want?" I shouted.

I gasped.

"What! Vera? Where are you? I want to see you. I must see you at once!"

My love was in dire distress. I could hear emotion in her voice. My heart beat quickly in my eagerness.

"Oh, come to me—do come to me!" she was saying hurriedly in a low tone, as though fearful of some one overhearing her. "I'm in such trouble, and you alone can help me. Tell me when you will come. Tell me quickly. At any moment someone may catch me talking on the telephone."

"Where are you? Give me your address, quickly," I answered, feverishly. I was madly anxious to meet her again.

"We are in London—but we go to Brighton—to-day—this afternoon—"

"Your address in London, quick."

"Twenty-six Upper—"

There was a sudden clatter. The receiver had been put back. Some one had interrupted her.

I tapped the little lever of the instrument repeatedly.

"Number, please," a monotonous voice asked.

"What number was I talking to this instant?" I said, almost trembling with anxiety.

"I'm sure I don't know. What number do you want?"

"The number I've been talking to."

"I tell you I don't know it," replied the female operator.

"Can't you find it out?"

"I'll try. Hold the line, please."

After a brief interval, the voice said—

"It may have been double-two two two Mayfair. Shall I ring them for you?"

"Please do."

I waited.

"You're through."

"Hello, what is it?" a beery voice asked.

"I want to speak to Miss Vera Thorold?"

"Vera 'oo?"

"Thorold."

"Theobald? He's out."

"*Thorold*, Miss *Vera Thorold*," I shouted in despair.

"Oh, we ain't got no Veras here," the beery voice replied, and I could picture the speaker's leer. "This ain't a ladies' seminary; it's Poulsen's Brewery Company, Limited. You're on the wrong number. Ring off."

And again the instrument was silent.

Vera had been cut off just at the moment she was about to reveal her whereabouts.

Almost beside myself with anxiety, I tried to collect my thoughts in order to devise some means of discovering Vera's whereabouts and getting into immediate communication with her. I even went to the telephone exchange, interviewed the manager, and told him the exact time, to the fraction of a minute, when I had been rung up, but though he did his best to help me, he could not trace the number.

I have a vivid imagination, and am of an exceptionally apprehensive disposition, which has led some men to declare that I meet trouble half-way, though that is a thing I am constantly warning my friends not to do. In this case, however, I found it impossible not to feel anxious, desperately anxious, about the one woman I really cared for in the whole world. She had appealed to me urgently for help, and I was impotent to help her.

Dejectedly I returned to my flat. The lift-boy was standing in the street, his hands in his pockets, the stump of a cheap cigarette between his lips. Without removing his hands from his pockets, or cigarette-end from his mouth, he looked up at me with an offensive grin, and jerked out the sentence between his teeth—

"There's a lady here to see you—a Miss Thorold."

"Miss Thorold? Where is she? How long has she been here?" I exclaimed, quelling all outward appearance of excitement.

"About ten minutes. She's up in your rooms, sir. She said you knew her, and she'd wait till you came back."

"Vera!" I gasped involuntarily, and entered the lift, frantic with impatience.

At last. She was there—in my rooms, awaiting me with explanation!

Chapter Five.

Puts Certain Questions.

Rarely have I felt more put out, or more bitterly disappointed, than I did when I hurried into my flat, expecting to come face to face with Vera, my beloved, and longing to take her in my arms to kiss and comfort her.

Instead, I was confronted by a spinster aunt of Vera's whom I had met only three times before, and to whom I had, the first time I was introduced to her—she insisted upon never remembering me either by name or by sight, and each time needing a fresh introduction—taken an ineradicable dislike.

"Ah, Mr Ashton, I'm so glad you've come," she said without rising. "I have called to talk to you about a great many things—I daresay you can guess what they are—about all this dreadful affair at Houghton."

Now the more annoyed I feel with anybody of my own social standing, the more coldly polite I invariably become. It was so on this occasion.

"I should love to stay and talk to you, Miss Thorold," I answered, after an instant's pause, "but I have just been sitting at the bedside of a sick friend. To-day is the first day he has been allowed to see anybody. The doctor said he ought not to have allowed me in so soon, and he warned me to go straight home, take off every stitch of clothing I have on, and send them at once to be disinfected."

"Oh, indeed?" she said rather nervously. "And what has been the matter with your friend?"

It was the question I wanted.

"Didn't I tell you?" I said. "It was smallpox."

My ruse proved even more successful than I had anticipated. Miss Thorold literally sprang to her feet, gathered up her satchel and umbrella, and with the hurried remark: "How perfectly monstrous—keep well away from me!" she edged her way round the wall to the door, and, calling to me from the little passage: "I will ring you on the telephone," went out of the flat, slamming the door after her.

But where was Vera? How could I discover her? I was beside myself with anxiety.

The Houghton affair created more than a nine days' wonder. The people of Rutland desperately resent anything in the nature of a scandal which casts a disagreeable reflection upon their county. I remember how some years ago they talked for months about an unpleasant affair to do with hunting.

"Even if it were true," some of the people who knew it to be true said one to another, "it ought never to have been exposed in that way. Think of the discredit it brings upon our county, and what a handle the Radicals and the Socialists will be able to make of it, if ever it is discovered that it really did occur."

And so it came about that, when I was called back to Oakham two days later, to attend the double inquest, many of the people there, with whom I had been on quite friendly terms, looked at me more or less askance. It is not well to make oneself notorious in a tiny county like Rutland, I quickly discovered, or even to become notorious through no fault of one's own.

Shall I ever forget how, at the inquest, questions put to me by all sorts of uneducated people upon whom the duty devolved of inquiring into the mysterious affair connected with Houghton Park?

I suppose it was because there was nobody else to question, that they cross-examined me so closely and so foolishly.

Their inquiries were endless. Had I known the Thorolds long? Could I name the date when I first became acquainted with them? Was it a fact that I rode Sir Charles' horses while I was a guest at Houghton? About how often did I ride them? And on how many days did I hunt during the fortnight I spent at Houghton?

All my replies were taken down in writing. Then came questions concerning my friendship with Miss Thorold, and these annoyed me considerably. Was the rumour that I was engaged to be married to her true? Was there any ground for the rumour? Was I at all attached to her? Was she attached to me? Had we ever corresponded by letter? Was it a fact that we called each other by our Christian names? Was it not true, that on one evening at least, we had smoked cigarettes together, alone in her boudoir?

It was. This admission seemed to gratify my cross-questioners considerably.

"And may I ask, Mr Ashton," asked a legal gentleman with a most offensive manner, as he looked me up and down, "if this took place with Sir Charles' knowledge?"

"Oh, yes it did. With his full knowledge and consent!"

"Oh, really. And you will pardon my asking, was Lady Thorold also aware that you and her daughter sat alone together late at night, smoking cigarettes and addressing each other by your Christian names?"

Now I am fairly even-tempered, but this local solicitor's objectionable insinuations ended by stirring me up. This, very likely, was what he desired that they should do.

"My dear sir," I exclaimed, "will you tell me if these questions of yours have any bearing at all upon the matter you are inquiring into, and if your very offensive innuendoes are intended as veiled, or rather as unveiled, insults to Miss Thorold or to myself?"

I heard some one near me murmur, "Hear, hear," at the back of the room. The comment encouraged me.

"You will not address me in that fashion again, please," my interlocutor answered hotly, reddening.

"In what fashion?"

"You will not call me 'your dear sir.' I object. I strongly object."

A titter of amusement trickled through the room. My adversary's fingers—for he had become an adversary—twitched.

"I was under the impression," he remarked pompously, "that I was addressing a gentleman."

I am not good at smart retorts, but I got one in when I answered him.

"A gentleman—I?" I exclaimed blandly. "I assure you, my dear sir, that I don't pose as a gentleman. I am quite a common man—just like yourself."

Considerable laughter greeted this remark, but it was at once suppressed. Still, I knew that this single quick rejoinder had biased "the gallery" in my favour. Common people enjoy witnessing the discomfiture of any individual in authority.

Two days later, I left Oakham and returned to London, feeling like a schoolboy going home for Christmas.

The days went by. On the following week I again went to Oakham to attend the adjourned inquest. In the case of the butler, an open verdict was returned, but in the case of the driver, one of murder by some person unknown.

Of Vera I had had no news.

"Twenty-six Upper..." That might be in London, or in Brighton. It might even be in some other town. I thought it probable, however, that the address she had been about to give was a London address, so I had spent the day before the inquest in trying the various London "Uppers" contained in "Kelly's Directory."

Heavens, what an array! When my eyes fell upon the list, my heart sank. For there were no less than fifty-four "Uppers" scattered about the Metropolis. Some, obviously, might be ruled out at once, or so I conjectured. Upper Street, Islington, for instance, close to the *Angel*, did not sound a likely "residential locality"—as the estate agents say—for people of Sir Charles and Lady Thorold's position to be staying in. Nor did Upper Bland near the *Elephant and Castle*, nor Upper Grange Road, off the Old Kent Road; nor Upper Chapman Street, Shadwell. On the other hand, Upper Brook Street; Upper George Street, Sloane Square; Upper Grosvenor Street, Park Lane; even Upper Phillimore Gardens, Kensington, seemed possible spots, and these and many other "Uppers" I tried, spinning from one to another in a taxi, until the driver began to look at me as though he had misgivings as to my sanity.

"Twenty-six don't seem to be your lucky number, sir," he said jocularly, when he had driven me to thirty-seven different "Uppers" and called in each at the house numbered twenty-six. "It wouldn't be twenty-six in some 'Lower' Street, or Place, or Road, or Gardens, would it, sir?"

He spoke only half in jest, but I resented his familiarity, and I told him so. His only comment, muttered beneath his breath, but loud enough for me to hear, was—

"Lummy! the cove's dotty in 'is own 'upper,' that's what *'ee* is."

On my return from Oakham I went to Brighton, wandering aimlessly about the streets and on the esplanade, hoping against hope that some fortunate turn in the wheel of Fate might bring me unexpectedly face to face with my sweet-faced beloved, whose prolonged and mysterious absence seemed to have made my heart grow fonder. Alas! fate only grinned at me ironically.

Vera had vanished with her family—entirely vanished.

But not wholly ironically. I had been distressed to find that the little silver flask picked up at Houghton had been mislaid. For hours I had hunted high and low for it in my flat. John had turned out all my clothes, and pulled the pockets inside out, and I had bullied him for his carelessness in losing it, and almost accused him of stealing it.

It was while in the train on my way back to London, after my second futile visit to Brighton, that I sat down on something hard. Almost at once I guessed what it was. Briefly, there had been a hole in the inside breast-pocket of my overcoat. It had been mended by John's wife—whose duty it was to keep all my clothes in order—before I knew of its existence. Therefore, when I had naturally enough suspected there being a hole in one of my pockets, and sought one, I had found all the pockets intact. The woman had mended the hole without noticing that the little flask, which had dropped through it, lay hidden in the bottom of the lining.

I ripped open the lining at once, and pulled out the flask, delighted at the discovery. And, as soon as I reached town, I took the flask to a chemist I knew and asked him to analyse its contents. He would do so without delay, he said, and let me know on the following morning the result of his analysis.

"It's a mixture of gelsiminum and ether," he said, as soon as I entered his shop next day.

"Poison, of course," I remarked.

He smiled.

"Well, I should rather think so," he answered drily. "A few drops would send a strong man to sleep for ever, and there is enough of the fluid here to send fifty men to sleep—for ever. Therefore one wouldn't exactly take it for one's health."

So here was a clue—of a sort. The first clue! My spirits rose. My next step must be to discover the owner of the flask, presumably some one with initials "D.P.," and the reason he—or she—had carried this fluid about.

I lunched at Brooks's, feeling more than usually bored by the members I met there. Several men whom I had not seen for several weeks were standing in front of the smoking-room fire, and as I entered, and they caught sight of me, they all grinned broadly.

"'The accused then left the Court with his friends,'" one of them said lightly, as I approached. "'He was granted a free pardon, but bound over in his own recognisances to keep the peace for six months.'"

"You *have* been getting yourself into trouble, Dick, and no mistake," observed his neighbour—I am generally called Dick by my friends.

"Into trouble? What do you mean?" I retorted, nettled.

"Why—you know quite well," he answered. "This Houghton affair, the scandal about the Thorolds, of course. How came you to get mixed up in it? We like you, old man, but you know it makes it a bit unpleasant for some of us. You know what people are. They will talk."

"I suppose you mean that men are judged by the company they keep, and that because I happened to be at Houghton at the time of that affair, and was unwillingly dragged into prominence by the newspapers, therefore that discredit reflects on me."

"Well, I should not have expressed it precisely in that way, but still—"

"Still what?"

"As you ask me, I suppose I must answer. I do think it rather unfortunate you should have got yourself mixed up in the business, and both Algie and Frank agree with me—don't you, Algie?" he ended, turning to his friend.

"Awe—er—awe—quite so, quite so. We were talking of you just as you came in, my dear old Dick, and we all agreed it was, awe—er—was—awe—a confounded pity you had anything to do with it. Bad form, you know, old Dick, all this notoriety. Never does to be unusual, singular, or different from other people—eh what? One's friends don't like it—and one don't like it oneself—what?"

Their shallow views and general mental vapidity, if I may put it so, jarred upon me. After spending ten minutes in their company, I went into the dining-room and lunched alone. Then I read the newspapers, dozed in an armchair for half-an-hour, and finally, at about four o'clock, returned to my flat in King Street. John met me on the stairs.

"Ah! there you are, sir," he exclaimed. "Did you meet them?"

"Meet whom?"

"Why, they haven't been gone not two minutes, so I thought you might have met them in the street, sir. They waited over half-an-hour."

"But who were they? What were their names?" I asked, irritated at John for not telling me at once the names of the visitors.

"A young lady and a gentleman—there's a card on your table, sir; I can't recall the names for the moment," he said, wrinkling his forehead as he scratched his ear to stimulate his memory. "The gentleman was extremely tall, quite a giant, with a dark beard."

I hurried up the stairs, for the lift was out of order, and let myself into my flat with my latch key. On the table, in my sitting-room, was a lady's card on a salver.

"Miss Thorold."

In Vera's handwriting were the words, scribbled in pencil across it—

"*So sorry we have missed you.*"

Chapter Six.

The House in the Square.

I admit that I was dumbfounded.

Vera and her mysterious friend were together, calling in the most matter-of-fact way possible, and just as though nothing had happened! It seemed incredible!

All at once a dreadful thought occurred to me that made me catch my breath. Was it possible that my love was an actress, in the sense that she was acting a part? Had she cruelly deceived me when she had declared so earnestly that she loved me? The reflection that, were she practising deception, she would not have come to see me thus openly with the man with the black beard, relieved my feelings only a little. For how came she to be with Davies at all? And again, who was this man Davies? Also that telephone message a fortnight previously, how could I account for it under the circumstances?

"Oh, come to me—do come to me! I am in such trouble," my love had cried so piteously, and then had added: "You alone can help me."

Some one else, apparently, must have helped her. Could it have been this big, dark man?

And was he, in consequence, supplanting me in her affection? The thought held me breathless.

At times I am something of a philosopher, though my relatives laugh when I tell them so, and reply, "Not a philosopher, only a well-meaning fellow, and extremely good-natured"—a description I detest. Realising now the uselessness of worrying over the matter, I decided to make no further move, but to sit quiet and await developments.

"If you worry," I often tell my friends, "it won't in the least help to avert impending disaster, while if what you worry about never comes to pass, you have made yourself unhappy to no purpose."

A platitude? Possibly. But two-thirds of the words of wisdom uttered by great men, and handed down as tradition to a worshipping posterity, are platitudes of the most commonplace type, if you really come to analyse them.

Time hung heavily. It generally ends by hanging heavily upon a man without occupation. But put yourself for a moment in my place. I had lost my love, and those days of inactivity and longing were doubly tedious because I ached to bestir myself somehow, anyhow, to clear up a mystery which, though gradually fading from the mind of a public ever athirst for fresh sensation, was actively alive in my own thoughts—the one thought, indeed, ever present in my mind. Why had the Thorolds so suddenly and mysteriously disappeared?

Thus it occurred to me, two days after Davies and Vera had called at my flat, to stroll down into Belgravia and interview the caretaker at 102, Belgrave Street. Possibly by this time, I reflected, he might have seen Sir Charles Thorold, or heard from him.

When I had rung three times, the door slowly opened to the length of its chain, and I think quite the queerest-looking little old man I had ever set eyes on, peered out. He gazed with his sharp, beady eyes up into my face for a moment or two, then asked, in a broken quavering voice—

"Are you another newspaper gen'leman?"

"Oh, no," I answered, laughing, for I guessed at once how he must have been harassed by reporters, and I could sympathise with him. "I am not a journalist—I'm only a gentleman."

Of course he was too old to note the satire, but the fact that I wore a silk hat and a clean collar, seemed to satisfy him that I must be a person of some consequence, and when I had assured him that I meant him no ill, but that, on the contrary, I might have something to tell him that he would like to hear, he shut the door, and I heard his trembling old hands remove the chain.

"And how long is it since Sir Charles was last here?" I said to him, when he had shown me into his little room on the ground floor, where a kettle purred on a gas-stove. "I know him well, you know; I was staying at Houghton Park when he disappeared."

He looked me up and down, surprised and apparently much interested.

"Were you indeed, sir?" he exclaimed. "Well, now—well, well!"

"Why don't you sit down and make yourself comfortable, my old friend," I went on affably. I drew forward his armchair, and he sank into it with a grunt of relief.

"You are a very kind gen'leman, you are, very kind indeed," he said, in a tone that betrayed true gratitude. "Ah! I've known gen'lemen in my time, and I know a gen'leman when I sees one, I do."

"What part of Norfolk do you come from?" I asked, as I took a seat near him, for I knew the Norfolk brogue quite well.

He looked at me and grinned.

"Well, now, that's strange you knowing I come from Norfolk! But it's true. Oh, yes, it is right. I'm a Norfolk man. I was born in Diss. I mind the time my father—"

"Yes, yes," I interrupted, "we'll talk about that presently," for I could see that, once allowed to start on the subject of his relatives and his native county, he would talk on for an hour. "What I have come here this afternoon to talk to you about is Sir Charles Thorold. When was he last here?"

"It will be near two years come Michaelmas," he answered, without an instant's hesitation. "And since then I haven't set eyes on him—I haven't."

"And has this house been shut up all the time?"

"Ay, all that time. I mind the time my father used to tell me—"

I damned his father under my breath, and quickly stopped him by asking who paid him his wages.

"My wages? Oh, Sir Charles' lawyers, Messrs Spink and Peters, of Lincoln's Inn, pays me my wages. But they are not going to pay me any more. No. They are not going to pay me any more now."

"Not going to pay you any more? What do you mean?"

"Give me notice to quit, they did, a week ago come Saturday."

"But why?"

"Orders from Sir Charles, they said. Would you like to see their letter, sir?"

"I should, if you have it by you."

It was brief, curt, and brutally frank—

"From Messrs Spink and Peters, Solicitors, 582, Lincoln's Inn, W.C.

"To William Taylor, Caretaker,—

"102, Belgrave Street, S.W.

"Messrs Spink and Peters are instructed by Sir Charles Thorold to inform William Taylor that owing to his advanced age his services will not be needed by Sir Charles Thorold after March 25. William Taylor is requested to acknowledge the receipt of this letter."

"They don't consider your feelings much," I said, as I refolded the letter and handed it back to him.

He seemed puzzled.

"Feelings, sir? What are those?" he asked. "I don't somehow seem to know."

"No matter. Under the circumstances it is, perhaps, as well you shouldn't know. Now, I want to ask you a few questions, my old friend—and look here, I am going, first of all, to make you a little present."

I slipped my fingers into my waistcoat pocket, produced a half-sovereign, and pressed it into the palm of his wrinkled old hand.

"To buy tobacco with—no, don't thank me," I said quickly, as he began to express gratitude. "Now, answer a few questions I am going to put to you. In the first place, how long have you been in Sir Charles' service?"

"Sixteen years, come Michaelmas," he answered promptly. "I came from Diss. I mind the time my father—"

"How did Sir Charles, or Mr Thorold as he was then, first hear of you?"

"He was in Downham Market. I was caretaker for the Reverend George Lattimer, and Sir Charles, I should say, Mr Thorold, came to see the house. I think he thought of buying it, but he didn't buy it. I showed him into every room, I remember, and as he was leaving he put his hand into his pocket, pulled out a sov'rin', and gave it to me, just as you have done. And then he said to me, he said: 'Ole man,' he said, 'would you like a better job than this?' Those were his very words, 'Ole man, would you like a better job than this?'"

He grinned and chuckled at the reflection, showing his toothless gums.

"And then he took you into his service. Did you come to London at once?"

"Ay, next week he brought me up, and I've been here ever since—in this house ever since. The Reverend George Lattimer wor vexed with Sir Charles for a 'stealing' me from his service, as he said. I mind in Diss, when—"

"Was there any reason why Mr Thorold should engage you in such a hurry? Did he give any reason? It seems strange he should have engaged a man of your age, living away in Norfolk, and brought you up to London at a few days' notice."

"Oh, yes there was reason—there was a reason."

"And what was it?"

"Well, well, it was not p'raps 'xactly what you might call a 'reason,' it was what Sir Charles he calls a 'stipilation.' 'I have a stipilation to make, Taylor,' he said, when he engaged me. 'Yes, sir,' I said, 'and what might this, this stipilation be?' I said. 'It's like this, Taylor,' he said. 'I'll engage you and pay you well, and you will come with me to Lundon to-morrow, and you shall have two comfortable rooms in my house,' those were his very words, sir, 'and you will have little work to do, 'cept when I am out of Lundon, and you have to look after the house and act as caretaker. But there be a stipilation I must make.' 'And what might that stipilation be, sir?' I asked him. 'It's like this,' he said, a looking rather hard at me. 'You must never see or know anything that goes on in my Lundon 'ouse, when I am there, or when I am not. If you see or hear anything, you must forget it. Do you understand? Do we understand each other?' he said. And I have done that, sir, ever since Sir Charles engaged me. Never have I seen what happened in this house, nor have I heard what happened in this house, nor known what happened in this house. I have kep' the stipilation, and I've served the master well."

"And for serving your master well, and doing your duty, you are rewarded by getting kicked out at a month's notice because of your 'advanced age.'"

The old man's eyes became suddenly moist as I said this, and I felt sorry I had spoken.

"Did you see or hear much you ought to have forgotten?" I hazarded, after a brief pause.

He peered up at me with an odd expression, then slowly shook his head.

"Have you actually forgotten all you saw and heard?" I inquired carelessly, as I lit a cigarette, "or do you only pretend?"

"I dusn't say, sir," he answered. "I dusn't say."

He looked to right and left, as it seemed to me instinctively, and as though to assure himself that no one else was present, that no one overheard him. It was evident to me that there was somebody he feared.

Several times I tried tactfully to "draw" him, but to no purpose.

"I should like to look over the house again," I said at last. "I know it well, for I stayed here often in days gone by, though I don't recollect ever seeing you here. How long is it since Sir Charles stayed here?"

"Three years come Lady Day," he answered.

"And has the house been empty ever since? Has it never been sub-let?"

"Never. Sir Charles never would sub-let it, though there were some who wanted it."

"Well, I will look over it, I think," I said, moving to rise. "I'm inclined to rent it myself; that's really why I am here."

He may, or may not, have believed the lie. Anyway, my suggestion filled him with alarm. He got up out of his chair.

"You can't, you can't," he exclaimed, greatly perturbed. He pushed his skinny hand into his jacket-pocket, and I heard him clutch his bunch of keys. "The doors are all locked—all locked."

"You have the keys; give them to me."

"I dusn't, I dusn't, indeed. All, you are a gen'leman, sir, you won't take the keys from an old man, sir, I know you won't."

"Sit down," I said, sharply.

Idle curiosity had prompted me to wish to go over the house. The old man's anxiety that I should not do so settled my determination. My thought travelled quickly.

"Have you a drop of anything to drink that you can give me?" I asked suddenly. "I should like a little whisky—or anything else will do."

Again the expression of dismay came into his old eyes.

"Don't tempt me, sir, ah, don't tempt me!" he exclaimed. "Sir Charles made me promise as long as I was with him I wouldn't touch a drop. I did once. Oh, I did once."

"And what happened?"

He hid his face in his hands, as if to shut out some horrid memory.

"Don't ask me what happened, sir, don't ask me. And I swore I wouldn't touch a drop again. And I haven't got a drop—except a cup of tea."

The kettle on the gas-stove had been boiling for some time. My intention—an evil one—when I had asked for something alcoholic, had been to induce the old man to drink with me until the effects of the whisky should cause him to overcome his scruples and hand over his keys. But tea!

At that moment my elbow rested on something hard in my pocket. Almost at the same moment an idea flashed into my brain. I tried to dispel it, but it wouldn't go. I allowed my mind to dwell upon it, and quickly it obsessed me.

Why, I don't know, but since the chemist had returned the little flask to me, after analysing its contents, I had carried it in my pocket constantly. It was there now. It was the flask that my elbow had pressed, recalling it to my mind.

"Twenty drops will send a strong man to sleep—for ever," he had said.

The words came back to me now. If it needed twenty drops to kill a strong man, surely a small dose could with safety be administered to a wiry little old man who, though decrepit, seemed still to possess considerable vitality. But would it be quite safe? Did I dare risk it?

"A cup of tea will do just as well," I said carelessly, tossing aside my cigarette. "No, don't you move. I see you have everything ready, and there are cups up on the shelf. Let me make the tea. I like tea made in one way only."

I felt quite guilty when he answered—

"You are very kind, sir; you are very kind; you are a gen'leman."

It was easily and quickly done. I had my back to him. I poured the tea into the cups. Then I let about five drops of the fluid in the flask fall into a spoon. I put the spoon into his cup, and stirred his tea with it.

In a few moments I saw he was growing drowsy. His bony chin dropped several times on to his chest, though he tried to keep awake. He muttered some unintelligible words. In a few minutes he was asleep.

I took his pulse. Yes, it was still quite strong. I waited a moment or two. Then, slipping my hand into his jacket-pocket, I took out the bunch of keys noiselessly, turned out the gas-stove, and stepped quietly out of the room, closing the door behind me.

Chapter Seven.

Treading among Shadows.

The house was found very dirty and neglected. It contained but little furniture. Dust lay thickly upon everything. The windows, I was almost tempted to think, had not been opened since Sir Charles had last lived there three years ago. There was also a damp, earthy smell in the hall.

As I went slowly up the stairs, bare of carpet or any other covering, they creaked and groaned in a way that was astonishing, for the houses in Belgrave Street are not so very old. The noises the stairs made echoed higher up.

I had decided to enter the rooms on the ground floor last of all. The first floor looked strangely unfamiliar. When last I had been here the house had been luxuriously furnished, and somehow the landing, in its naked state, seemed larger than when I remembered it.

Ah! What fun we had had in that house long ago!

My friends the Thorolds had entertained largely, and their acquaintances had all been bright, amusing people, so different, as I had sometimes told my friends, from the colourless, stupid folk whose company one so often has to endure when staying in the houses of acquaintances. I often think, when mixing with such people, of the story of the two women discussing a certain "impossible" young man, of a type one meets frequently.

"How deadly dull Bertie Fairbairn is," one of them said. "He never talks at all."

"Oh, he is better than his brother Reggie," the other answered. "Whenever you speak to Bertie he says, 'Right O!'"

The door of the apartment that had been the large drawing-room was locked. On the bunch of keys, I soon found the key that fitted, and I entered.

Phew, what a musty smell! Most oppressive. The blinds were drawn half-way down the windows and, by the look of them, had been so for some considerable time. The furniture that remained was all hidden under holland sheets, and the pictures on the walls, draped in dust-proof coverings, looked like the slabs of salted beef, and the sides of smoke-cured pork one sees hung in some farmhouses. The carpets were dusty, moth-eaten and rotten.

Gingerly, with thumb and forefinger, I picked up the corners of some of the furniture coverings. There was nothing but the furniture underneath, except in one instance, where I saw, upon an easy-chair, a plate with some mouldy remnants of food upon it. No wonder the atmosphere was foetid.

I was about to leave the room, glad to get out of it, when I noticed in a corner of the ceiling a dark, yellow-brown stain, about a yard in circumference. This struck me as curious, and I went over and stood under it, and gazed up at it, endeavouring to discover its origin. Then I saw that it was moist. I pulled up one of the blinds in order to see better, but my scrutiny failed to give me any inkling as to the origin of the stain.

I went out, shut and locked the door, and entered several other rooms, the doors of all of which I found locked. One room was very like another, the only difference being that the smell in some was closer and nastier than the smell in others, though all the smells had, what I may call the same "flavour"—a "taste" of dry rot. I wondered if Sir Charles knew how his house was being neglected, how dirt and dust were being allowed to accumulate.

This was Lady Thorold's boudoir, if I remembered aright. The inside of the lock was so rusty that I had difficulty in turning the key. Everything shrouded, as elsewhere, but, judging from the odd projections in the coverings, I concluded that ornaments and bric-à-brac had been left upon the tables.

Nor was I mistaken. As I lifted the cloths and dust sheets, objects that I remembered seeing set about the room in the old days, became revealed. There were several beautiful statues, priceless pieces of antique furniture from Naples and Florence, curious carved wooden figures that Sir Charles had collected during his travels in the Southern Pacific, cloisonné vases from Tokio and Osaka, a barely decent sculpture bought by Sir Charles from a Japanese witch-doctor who lived a hermit's life on an island in the Inland Sea—how well I remembered Lady Thorold's emphatic disapproval of this figure, and her objection to her husband's displaying it in the way he did— treasures from different parts of China, from New Guinea, Burmah, the West Indies and elsewhere.

Another cloth I lifted. Beneath it were a number of photographs in frames, piled faces downward in heaps. I picked up some of them, and took them out to look at. A picture of Vera in a short frock, with a teddy-bear tucked under her arm, interested me; so did a portrait of Lady Thorold dressed in a fashion long since past; and so did a portrait of my old father in his Guards uniform. The rest were portraits of people I didn't know. I looked at one or two more, and was about to replace the frames where I had found them, when I turned up one that startled me.

It was a cabinet, in a bog-oak frame, of the man whose likeness had caused the commotion at Houghton, the man who had called himself Smithson. But it was not a portrait similar to the one I had taken away. The same man, undoubtedly, but in a different attitude, and apparently many years younger.

Closely I scrutinised it.

The enigma presented was complete. I am not a pilferer, but I considered that I should be justified in putting the portrait into my pocket, and I did so without another thought. Then I replaced all the frames where I had found them, and resumed my ramble over the house.

In the rest of the rooms on that floor, I found nothing further of interest. On the floor above, however, a surprise was in store for me.

The first two rooms were bedrooms, neglected-looking and very dusty. There were fewer coverings here. Dust was upon the floor, on the beds, on the chairs and tables, on the window-sills, on the wash-stands, on the chests of drawers, on the mantelpiece—everywhere. In the next room, the door of which I was surprised to find unlocked, just the same. A table of dark mahogany was thickly coated with dust.

Hullo! Why, what was this? I thought at once of a detective friend of mine, and wondered what he would have said, what opinion he would have formed and what conclusion he would have come to, had he been in my place at that moment. For on the table, close to the edge of it, was the clear outline of a hand. Someone had quite recently—apparently within the last few hours, and certainly since the previous day—put his hand upon that dusty table. I scanned the outline closely; then suddenly I started.

There could be no doubt whatever—it was not the outline of Taylor's hand. The fingers that had rested there were long and tapering. This was not the impression of a man's hand, but of a woman's—of a woman's left hand.

Evidently some one had been in this room recently. From point to point I walked, looking for further traces, but there were none that I could see. What woman could have been in here so lately? And did the old man asleep downstairs know of her entry? He must have, for she could not have entered the house, had he not admitted her. I felt I was becoming quite a clever detective, with an exceptional gift for deduction from the obvious. Another gleam of intelligence led me to conclude that this woman's presence in the house probably accounted for Taylor's determination not to let me go over the house.

I thought I heard a sound. I held my breath and stood still, listening intently, but the only sound that came to me was the distant shrill whistle of some one summoning a taxi. Outside in the passage, all was still as death. I walked to the end of the passage, peeped into other bedrooms, then returned to the room with the table bearing the imprint of the hand.

The windows overlooked Belgrave Street—double windows, which made the sound of the traffic down below inaudible. Carelessly I watched for some moments the vehicles and passers-by, unconsciously striving to puzzle out, meanwhile, the problem of the hand. Suddenly, two figures approaching along the pavement from the direction of Wilton Street, arrested my attention. They seemed familiar to me. As they came nearer, a strange feeling of excitement possessed me, for I recognised the burly form of Davies, or "Smithson," and as he had called himself, and, walking beside him, Sir Charles Thorold. The two appeared to be engaged in earnest conversation.

They disappeared where the street turned, and as I came away from the window I noticed, for the first time, that the room had another door, a door leading presumably into a dressing-room. I went over to it. It was locked.

I tried a key on the bunch, but at once discovered that a key was in the door. The door was locked on the inside!

I knocked. There was no answer. And just then I distinctly heard a sound inside the room.

"Who's there?" I called out. "Let me in!"

A sound, resembling a sob, reached me faintly. I heard light footfalls. The key turned slowly, and the lock clicked.

I turned the handle, and went in.

Chapter Eight.

More Mystery.

I halted on the threshold, wondering and aghast.

Vera, in her hat and jacket, stood facing me a few yards away. She was extremely pale. There were dark shadows under her eyes, and I saw at once she had been weeping.

For a moment neither of us spoke. Then, pulling myself together—

"Why, darling, what are you doing here?" I asked.

She did not answer. Her big, blue, unfathomable eyes were set on mine. There was in them an expression I had not seen there before—an odd, unnatural look, which made me feel uncomfortable.

"What are you doing here?" I repeated. "Why did you call upon me with Davies?"

Her lips moved, but no words came. I went over and took her hand. It was quite cold.

Suddenly she spoke slowly, and hoarsely, but like some one in a trance.

"I cannot tell you," she said simply. "I wanted to see you."

"Oh, but you *must*!"

Her eyes met mine, and I saw her arched brows contract slightly.

"Nobody says, 'must' to me," she answered, in a tone that chilled me.

"Vera! Vera!" I exclaimed, dismayed at her strange manner, "what is the matter? What has happened to you, darling? Why are you like this? Don't you need my help now? You told me on the telephone that you did."

"On the telephone? When was that?"

"Why, not three weeks ago. Surely you remember? It was the last time we spoke to each other. You had begun to tell me your address, when suddenly we were cut off."

I saw her knit her brows, as though trying to remember. Then, all at once, memory seemed to return.

"Ah, yes," she exclaimed, more in her ordinary voice. "I recollect. I wanted your help then. I needed it badly, but now—"

"Well, what?" I said anxiously, as she checked herself.

"It's too late—now," she whispered. My arm was about her thin waist, and I felt that she shuddered.

"Vera, what has happened? Tell me—oh, tell me, dearest!"

I took both her small hands in mine. I was seriously alarmed, for there was a strange light in her eyes.

"Why did you not come when I wanted you?" she asked, bitterly.

"I would have, but how could I without knowing where you were?"

She paused in indecision.

"I'm sorry. You are too late, Dick," and she shook her head mournfully.

"Oh, don't say that," I cried, not knowing what to think. "Has some misfortune befallen you? Tell me what it is. You surely know that you can trust me."

"Trust *you*!"

There was bitterness, nay mockery, in her voice.

"Good heavens, yes! Why not?" I cried.

"There is no one in whom I can trust. I can trust you, Mr Ashton, least of all—now."

Evidently she was labouring under some terrible delusion. Had some one slandered me—poisoned her mind against me?

"How long have you been here?" I asked suddenly, thinking it best to change the subject for the moment.

"Since early this morning," she answered at once.

"Did you come here alone?"

"Alone? No, he brought me."

"'He?' Who is 'he'?"

"Dago Paulton."

"Dago Paulton?" I echoed. "Is he the man Smithson?" I asked shrewdly.

"Of course. Who else did you suppose?" Then, suddenly, her expression changed to one of surprise.

"But you don't know him, surely," she exclaimed. "You have never even met him. He told me so himself."

"No, but I know about him," I said, with recollection crowding upon me.

"You don't! You cannot! Who told you about him? And what did they tell you? Oh, this is awful, it is worse than I feared," she exclaimed, in great distress. "And now it is all too late."

"Too late for what? To do what?"

"To help me. To save me from him."

"Does this man want to marry you?"

"He is going to. He *must* marry me. Ah! You don't know—you—"

My love shuddered, without completing her sentence.

"Why? Is it to save your father?" I hazarded again.

"To save my father—and my mother," she exclaimed. And then, to my surprise, she sank upon a chair, flung her arms out upon the table in front of her, hid her face up on them, and began to sob hysterically.

"Vera, my dearest, don't—oh! don't," I said beseechingly, as I bent down, put an arm tenderly about her, and kissed her upon the cheek. "Don't cry like that, darling. It's never too late, until a misfortune has really happened. You are not married to him. There may be a way of escape. Trust me. Treat me as a friend—we have been friends so long—tell me everything, and I will try to help you out of all your trouble."

She started up.

"Trust you!" she burst forth, her face flushed. "Can I trust any one?"

"I've done nothing; I don't know what you mean, or to what you refer!" I exclaimed blankly.

"Can you look at me like that," she said slowly, after a pause, "and tell me, upon your oath, that you did not reveal my father's secret; that you have never revealed it to anybody—never in your life?"

"I give you my solemn oath, Vera, that I have never in my life revealed it to anybody, or hinted at it, or said anything, either consciously or unconsciously, that might have led any one to suspect," I answered fervently, with my eyes fixed on hers.

Truth to tell, I had not the remotest idea what the secret was, nor, until this instant, had it ever occurred to me to think that Sir Charles possessed a secret. I felt, however, that I had a part to play, and I was determined to play it to the best of my ability. Vera seemed to take it quite for granted that I knew her father's secret, and I felt instinctively that, were I to endeavour to assure her that I was in complete ignorance of everything, she would not, under the circumstances, believe a single word I said.

"Do you believe me now?" I asked, as she did not speak.

"Yes—I do believe you," was her slow response. And then she let me take her in my ready arms again.

She seemed to have been suddenly relieved of a great weight, and now she spoke in quite her ordinary way.

"Where is Paulton now?" was my next question. At last there seemed to be some remote possibility of the tangle of past events becoming gradually unravelled. I knew, however, that I was treading thin ice. A single careless word might lead her to suspect my duplicity. In a sense, I was still groping in the dark, pretending that I knew a great deal, whereas I knew nothing.

"He is coming to-night to fetch me."

"At what time?"

"At ten o'clock."

"And you are to wait here until then?"

"Yes."

"What have you had to eat?"

"Some tea, and bread and butter," and she glanced towards a table, on which stood a teapot and an empty plate.

"You can't subsist on that," I said quickly.

"More food is to be brought to me by old Taylor at five o'clock."

I glanced at my watch. It was a quarter-past four.

"Why don't you go out and go away?" I suggested. "There is surely nothing to prevent you. Why do you remain here in helpless inactivity?"

"Where should I go? I haven't any money. I haven't a sou. Besides—besides—I dare not disobey. If I did, he—he'd—he'd bring disaster—terrible disaster, upon me!"

"I can lend you some money," I said. Then a thought struck me.

"Why not come away with me?" I exclaimed. "I will get you a room at an hotel, see to you, provide you with money, and take care that nobody objectionable—neither this fellow Paulton, nor anybody else—molests you."

"Ah, Dick, if only I dared!" she exclaimed fervently, with shining eyes.

"You love me, Vera—do you not?"

"You know that I do, Dick."

"Then leave here. Who is to prevent you? Where are your father and mother?"

She turned sharply.

"How can you ask that?" she cried, with a quick glance. I pulled myself together on the instant. I was forgetting to be cautious.

"Wouldn't it be safe for you to appeal to them for help?" I asked vaguely.

She paused, evidently reflecting, and I breathed more freely.

"Under the circumstances—no," she said at last, with decision. "They must await developments. I must remain here. Listen! What was that?" And she started in fear.

The door stood ajar. The door of the room I had been in, which opened on to the passage, was also open. Both of us listened intently. The sound of men's voices, somewhere in the house, became audible.

I crept out into the passage on tiptoe, walked a little distance along it, stopped, and listened again. Yes, there were voices in the hall. Two men were talking. At once I recognised that Sir Charles Thorold, and the man known as Davies, were engaged in earnest conversation in low tones. In the otherwise silent and deserted house, their words were distinctly audible.

"We must get a doctor—we must," I heard the big fellow say deeply. "I thought at first the fellow was asleep, then that he was drunk. The pulse is hardly perceptible."

"But how can we?" Thorold answered. "It isn't safe. There would be inquiries, and if he should die there would surely be an inquest, and then—"

He dropped his voice, and I could not catch the last words. Then Davies again spoke.

"I found this umbrella, and these gloves, on the table in his room," I heard him say, "and there are two tea-cups on the table. Both have been used, used within the last half-hour, I should say. The tea in them is still warm, and the teapot is quite hot." My heart stopped its beating. I put out an arm to support myself. A slight feeling of giddiness came over me. I broke out into a cold perspiration, for I had left my gloves and umbrella in the old man's room!

My mouth turned suddenly dry, as I thought of the tea I had doctored with the drops from the flask, of which only a little was needed to send "a strong man to sleep—for ever."

But Davies and Sir Charles were talking again, so I pulled myself together.

"How do you account for this umbrella and the gloves?" I heard Davies ask, and Thorold answered: "Let me have a look at them."

They were silent for some moments.

"He has had some one there, that's evident," Sir Charles said. "Who on earth can it have been? This is an expensive umbrella, silk, and gold-mounted, and these gloves, too, are good ones. It's extraordinary their owner should have forgotten to take them with him."

"He may be in the house still," answered Davies. "I hope, for his own sake, he isn't," Sir Charles said, in a hard voice. "Let us come and have a look at poor old Taylor. We shall find the keys in his pocket, anyway, and when we have attended to the other matter, we'll go up and see Vera, and try to bring her to her senses with regard to Paulton. She must do it—hang it—she *must*! I hate the thought of it, but it's my only chance of escape from this accursed parasite!"

Voices and footsteps died away. Once more the house was silent as death.

Truly, that deserted house was a house of mystery.

Chapter Nine.

The Gentleman Named Paulton.

On creeping back to her room, I found Vera awaiting me anxiously.

She, too, had heard the men talking, she had recognised her father's and his companion's voices, though unable to catch what was being said. I bent, and we exchanged kisses. In a few words I told her what had occurred, and explained the situation. I wanted to ask her about the man Davies; how she came to know him, and if she had known him long. There were other matters, too, that I wished to talk to her about, but there was no time to do so then.

Though I pride myself upon a rapidity of decision in moments of crises, and have misled the more ingenuous among my friends into believing that I really am a man of exceedingly strong character, who would never find himself at a loss if brought suddenly face to face with a critical problem, I don't mind admitting that I am an invertebrate, vacillating creature at such times. Oh, no, I never lose my head. Don't think that. But when instant decision is needed, and there are several decisions one might come to, I get quite "jumpy," half make up my mind to take one course, half make up my mind to take the opposite course, and finally take the third, or it may be the fourth or fifth.

"Well, you had better get away at once, dear," Vera urged quickly, when I had told her what I had heard below.

"But what are you going to do?" I asked.

"Oh, I know what I'm going to do," she replied at once, "but I want to have your plan. I know, dear, you are never at a loss when 'up against it,' to use your own phrase. You have often told me so, or implied it."

Now I did not entirely like her tone. There was a curious gleam in her eyes, which I mistrusted. I had noticed that gleam before, on occasions when she had been drawing people on to make admissions that they did not wish to make. She was rather too fond, I had sometimes thought, of indulging in a form of intellectual pastime that I have heard people who talk slang—a thing that I detest—call "pulling you by the leg." The suspicion crossed my mind at that moment, that Vera was trying to "pull my leg"—and I frankly didn't like it.

"This is no time for joking, Vera," I said, for the "gleam" in her eyes had now become a twinkle. "This is a time for action—and very prompt action."

I wondered how she could jest at such a moment. "That is why I want you to act," she answered innocently, "and to act promptly. However, as I believe you have no idea what to do, Dick, I'm going to tell you what to do, and you must do it—promptly. Now, follow me. I know my way about this place."

She led me softly along the corridor, turned to the right, then to the left, and then to the left again. Presently we reached the top of a flight of steep, and very narrow wooden stairs.

"Follow me," she whispered again, "and keep one hand on that rope," indicating a cord that served as a bannister. "These stairs are slippery, or they always used to be. As a child, I used to fall down them every Sunday."

We were on the first floor. The stairs continued to the ground floor. She turned suddenly.

"How about your gloves and umbrella?"

There was the curious look in her eyes again, so I paid no attention.

"Have you matches?" she asked, a moment later.

I struck one, and, stooping, we made our way along a narrow, dark passage, with a low ceiling. Five stone steps down into a damp, stone tunnel, about twenty feet in length, then to the right, and we came to a wooden door.

"Give me your keys," she said.

I did so, and she unlocked the door. It led into a little stone-flagged yard. On three sides of it were high walls, walls of houses. The wall on the fourth side, only a few feet high, was surmounted by iron rails. Stone steps led up to the gate at the end of the rails. She opened the gate, re-locking it when we had passed out, and we stood in a stone-flagged cul-de-sac, about fifteen yards long, across the open end of which, the traffic of the street could be seen passing to and fro.

"And now," she said, when we had reached the street, disobeying the injunction of Paulton, "you are going to tell me what I must do next."

I hailed a taxi, and we drove off in it, discussing plans as we went along.

Then I secured a room for her in a comfortable little hotel I knew of, in a street off Russell Square. The difficulty that now arose, was how to get her luggage.

She told me all her things were packed, as she was to have left for Paris that night, alone. The order received from her father was, that she should remain in an obscure lodging near Rue la Harpe, the address of which, he had given her. There she would receive further instructions. These instructions, she told me, were to come either from her father, or from Paulton. She had strict orders not to communicate with Davies. Her luggage was in Brighton. Sir Charles and Lady Thorold had been staying in Brighton, and she had come up that morning. Paulton had met her at Victoria, and taken her in a cab direct to her father's empty house in Belgrave Street. He had told her that if she dared go out before he came to her at ten that night, he would go to the police.

"But who is this man Davies?" I asked.

"A friend."

"But cannot you tell me something more concerning him?" I demanded.

"At present, no. I regret, Dick, that I am not allowed to say anything—my lips are sealed."

"And Paulton. Why obey him so subserviently?"

"Ah!" she sighed. "Because I am compelled."

With these rebuffs, I was forced to be satisfied.

With regard to the plan for recovering her luggage, I rose to the occasion. After pondering the problem for a quarter of an hour, I suggested that she should write a note to her mother in Brighton, saying that Paulton had suddenly changed his plans, and that her luggage was wanted at once. It was to have been sent off at eight o'clock that night, when Paulton would meet it at Victoria, she had told me. The bearer of the note we would now send to Brighton—a District Messenger—would be instructed to bring the luggage back with him. I looked up the trains in the railway-guide, and found it would be just possible for the messenger to do this in the time. To avoid any mishap, I told the messenger to alight, on his return journey, at Clapham Junction, and bring the luggage from there, in a taxi, to the hotel near Russell Square.

We dined together upstairs, at the *Trocadero*—ah! how I enjoyed that evening! How delightful it was to sit *tête-à-tête* with her. Before we had finished dinner, word was brought to us that Vera's luggage had arrived.

"I think I managed that rather well," I said. "Don't you?"

"No," she answered, "I don't."

"No?"

"As you ask me, I may as well tell you that I think you could hardly have 'managed' it worse. You have simply put Paulton on my track."

"But how?"

"How! Really, my dear Dick, your intelligence resembles a child's. You send a messenger for my luggage. Acting on your instructions, he brings it from Brighton to Clapham Junction by train, then hails a taxi, and brings the luggage on it direct to this hotel. Paulton is told by my mother in Brighton, that a messenger from London called for the luggage. All he has to do, is to ring up the messenger offices, until he finds the one where you engaged your messenger. Having found that out, he ascertains from the messenger the address to which he took the luggage in the taxi, and at once he comes and finds me."

"But," I said quickly, "Paulton is not in Brighton."

"How can that matter? He can easily find out who took my luggage. I tell you, dear, if Paulton finds me, worse still, if he finds me with you, the result will be terrible for all of us. You should yourself have gone to Clapham, met the messenger-boy there, and yourself have brought the luggage here."

I felt crushed. I had believed my plan had been laid so cleverly. At the same time, my admiration for Vera's foresight increased, though I did not tell her so.

We went back to the hotel at once, took away the luggage with us, and by ten o'clock that night she was comfortably settled in another small hotel, within a stone's throw of Hampstead Heath.

My sweet-faced, well-beloved told me many things I wanted to know, but alas! not everything, and all the time we conversed, I had to bear in mind the important fact that she believed me to be familiar with Sir Charles' secret—the secret that had led to his sudden flight from Houghton with her mother, herself and the French maid. I mistrusted that French maid—Judith. I had disliked the tone in which she had addressed Vera, when she had called her away from me that night at Houghton, and told her that Lady Thorold wanted her. I had noticed the maid on one or two previous occasions, and from the first I had disliked her. Her voice was so smooth, her manner so artificially deferential, and altogether she had seemed to me stealthy and cat-like. I believed her to be a hypocrite, if not a schemer.

The man who had called himself Davies, Vera told me, in the course of our long conversation that evening, was not named Smithson at all. That was a name he had adopted for some motive which, she seemed to take it for granted, I must be able to guess. Mexican by birth, though of British-Portuguese parentage, he had spoken to her, perhaps, half-a-dozen times. He appeared to be a friend of her father, she said, though what interest they had in common she had never been able to discover.

Speaking of Paulton, she said, her soft hand resting in mine, that he had known her mother longer than her father, and he had, she believed, been introduced by her mother to Sir Charles, since which time, the two men's intimacy had steadily increased.

She gave no reason for the dismay the sight of the framed panel portrait of "Smithson" had created, or for the sudden dismissal that night of all the servants at Houghton, and the subsequent flight. I could not quite decide, in my mind, if she took it for granted that I, knowing Sir Charles' secret—as she supposed—knew also why he had left Houghton thus mysteriously, or whether she intentionally refrained from telling me. But certainly she seemed to think there was no reason to tell me who had done poor James, the butler, to death, or who had fired the rifle shots from the wood, and killed the chauffeur. At the inquest on the butler, the jury had returned an open verdict.

Could he have been drowned by Paulton, and drowned intentionally? Or was Davies responsible for his death? That it must have been one of those two men I now felt certain—supposing he had not committed suicide, or been drowned by accident.

Another thing Vera clearly took for granted was, that I must have known why the man hidden in the wood had fired those shots at me. I had guessed, of course, from the first, that the bullet that had killed the driver had been meant for me; though why anybody should wish to do me harm I had not the remotest idea.

Of some points, of course, my love was ignorant as myself.

On the subject of the flask with the gelsiminum—a very potent poison distilled from the root of the yellow jasmine—that had been picked up on the drive at Houghton, just outside the front door, Vera said nothing. Indeed, though I referred to it more than once, she each time turned the conversation into a different channel, as though by accident.

"By the way, darling," I said, as our lips met again in a long, lingering caress, when we had been talking a long time, "why did you ring me up to tell me you were in trouble and needed my help, and why did you call with Davies at my chambers?"

Several times during the evening I had been on the point of asking her these questions, but on each occasion she had diverted my intention. It seemed odd, too, that though I had more than once asked her to tell me Davies' true name, she had each time turned the conversation without satisfying me. And at last she had point-blank refused to tell me.

Why? I wondered.

She looked at me steadily for some moments.

"It seems almost incredible, Dick," she said at last, speaking very slowly, and drawing herself away, "that knowing my father's secret, you should ask those questions. Tell me, how did you come to make the terrible discovery about my father? How long have you known everything? Who told you about it?"

Chapter Ten.

Relates a Strange Incident.

Vera's very direct questions took me aback, though I had expected them sooner or later. "Who told me?" I said, echoing the words in order to gain time for thought, my arms still about her. "Oh, I'm sure I can't remember. I seem to have known it a long time."

"It can't have been such a *very* long time," she answered, still looking at me in that queer way that made me feel uncomfortable. "Surely you must remember who told you. It is hardly the sort of thing one would be told every day—or even twice in one's life, is it?"

"Honestly," I said with quick decision, "I can't tell you how I came to know it."

"Your 'cannot' means 'will not,'" she said, and her lip twitched in the curious way that I knew meant she was nettled.

However, after that she dropped the subject, and I felt relieved. I hated deceiving her, yet I was compelled. I am not an adept in the art of what Lamb calls "walking round about a truth," at least, not for more than a minute or two at a time, and my love had such quick intelligence that it is no easy matter—as I had several times discovered, to my discomfiture—to mislead her.

For the first time since we had met in the house in Belgrave Street, our conversation became purely personal.

I had almost feared the events of the past weeks might have altered her regard for me, and it afforded me intense relief to find I was mistaken. For I was desperately in love with her, more so than I cared to admit even to myself. And now I found to my joy that my love for her was apparently fully reciprocated.

And yet why should she care for me? This puzzled me, I confess, though I know as a thoroughgoing man of the world and as a cosmopolitan that women do take most curious likes and dislikes. I am neither clever, good-looking nor amusing, nor, I believe, even particularly "good company" as it is called. There are scores upon scores of men just like myself. You meet them everywhere, in town and in the country. Society teems with them, and our clubs are full of them. Men, young and middle aged, who have been educated at the public schools and Universities, who have comfortable incomes, are fond of sport, who travel up and down Europe, who have never in their lives done a stroke of work—and don't intend ever to do one if they can help it—who live solely for amusement and for the pleasure of living.

What do women see in such men, women who have plenty of money and therefore do not need to marry in order to secure a home or to better themselves? What did—what could Vera Thorold see in me to attract her, least of all to tempt her to wish to marry me?

"Vera, my dearest," I said, when we had talked of each other's affairs for a considerable time, "why not marry me now? I can get a special licence! Then you will be free of all trouble, and nobody will be able to molest you. I shall have a right to protect you in every way possible."

"Free of all trouble if I marry you, Richard?" she answered, reflectively, evading my question, and looking at me queerly.

"And why not?" I asked. I felt rather hurt, for her words seemed to imply some hidden meaning. "Don't you think I shall be good to you and treat you properly?"

"Oh, that would be all right," she answered, apparently amused at my misconstruing her meaning. "I am sure, Dick, that you would be good to any girl. I have already heard of your spoiling two or three girls, and giving them presents they had no right to accept from you—eh?" she asked mischievously.

I am afraid I turned rather red, for, to be candid, I am something of a fool where women are concerned. At the same time I was surprised at her knowing the truth, and I suppose she guessed this, for, before I had time to speak again, she went on—

"You must not forget that I am a modern girl, my dear old Dick. I know a great deal that I suppose I have no business to know, and when I hear things I remember them. Don't for a moment flatter yourself that I think you perfect. I don't. My frank opinion of you is that you really are an awfully good sort, kind, sympathetic, unselfish—singularly unselfish for a man—generous to a fault, and extravagant. In short, I like you far, far better than any man I have ever met, and I love you very much, you dear old boy—but there it ends."

"I should rather say it did!" I answered. "If you really think all that of me, I am more than satisfied."

"On the other hand," she continued quickly, "I don't pretend to think—and you needn't think I do—that you are not just like most other men in some respects, in one respect in particular."

"What is the one respect?"

"You are dreadfully susceptible—oh, yes, Dick, you are! There is no need for any one to tell me that. I can see it in your face. Your eyes betray you. You have what I once heard a girl friend of mine call, 'affectionate eyes.' She said to me: 'Never trust a man who has "affectionate eyes," and I never have trusted one—except you.'"

"I am flattered dear. Then why not do what I suggest?" I asked, raising her soft hand to my lips.

"It wouldn't be safe, Dick, it really wouldn't. We must wait until—until Paulton is dead."

"Until Paulton—is—until he—is dead!" I gasped. "Good Heavens! that may not be for years!"

She smiled oddly.

"He may live for years, of course," she answered drily.

"What do you mean?" I asked, staring at her in amazement.

"I mean," she said, looking straight at me, and her voice suddenly grew hard, "that when he is dead, the world will be rid of a creature who ought never to have been born."

Her eyes blazed.

"Ah! Dick—Ah! Dick!" she went on with extraordinary force, sighing heavily, "if you only knew the life that man has led—the misery he has caused, the horrors that are traceable to his vile diabolical plots. My father and mother are only two of his many victims. He is a man I dread. I am not a coward, no one can call me that, but—but I fear Dago Paulton—I fear him terribly." She was trembling in my arms, though whether through fear, or only from emotion, I could not say. Nor could I think of any apt words which might soothe her, except to say—

"Leave him to me, dearest. Yet from what you tell me," I said after a pause, "I can only suppose that some one is—how shall I put it?—going to encompass Paulton's death."

"Who knows?" she asked vaguely, looking up into my eyes.

I shrugged my shoulders, but said nothing. There was nothing I could say. This much I had suspected at any rate—Paulton had been responsible for the chauffeur's death—or Vera believed him to have been.

When I left my beloved late that night, and returned to King Street, I was not satisfied with my discoveries. So many mysteries still remained unsolved. What was the danger that had threatened her when she had rung me up at my flat, and begged me to help her? Where had she been staying? What danger threatened her now? What hold had the man Paulton over her, and why did she fear to disobey him? Most perplexing of all—what was her father's secret, and why had he fled from Houghton?

There were many minor problems, too, which still needed solution. Who was Davies; what was his true name, and why was he so intimate with Sir Charles?

Again I seemed to see that curious stain on the ceiling of the room in Belgrave Street, and once more I wondered what had caused it. It might be, of course, merely a stain caused by some leaking pipe, and yet—

I thought of that remarkable conversation I had heard in the hall of the unoccupied house. What had they meant when they said they must "bring Vera to her senses"? Also, why had they seemed averse from calling in a doctor to see the old man Taylor, and to—

Taylor! I had been so much engrossed with Vera and her bondage of terror for the past few hours that I had forgotten all about him. Taylor. Had he recovered consciousness, I wondered, or had he—

A cold shiver ran through me as this last thought occurred to me.

It must have been quite two o'clock in the morning before I fell asleep. I am not an early riser, and my first feeling when I was awakened by John shaking me rather roughly, was one of annoyance. With difficulty I roused myself thoroughly. My servant was standing by the bedside, looking very pale.

"There are two police-officers downstairs," he said huskily. "They have come—they say they have come, sir—"

"Well, out with it," I exclaimed wrathfully, as he checked himself abruptly. "What have they come for? Do they want to see me?"

He braced himself with an effort—

"They say, sir," he answered, "that—that they've come to arrest you! It is something to do, I think, with some old man who's been found dead in an unoccupied 'ouse."

Chapter Eleven.

Contains some Strange News.

My heart seemed to stop beating. Old Taylor, then, was dead, and I sat up in bed, staring straight before me.

For nearly a minute I did not speak. All the time I felt John's calm gaze, puzzled, inquisitive, fixed upon me. I had gone through enough unhappiness during these past weeks to last me a lifetime, but all that I had endured would be as nothing by comparison with this. I could not blind myself to one fact—I had poisoned old Taylor deliberately. Had I, by some hideous miscalculation, the result of ignorance, overdosed him, and brought his poor old life to a premature end? I might be charged with manslaughter. Or worse!

Why! I might be convicted of murder. I might even be hanged! The grim thought held me breathless.

And Vera—my thoughts fled to her at once—what would become of Vera? Even if I were only imprisoned, and only for a short spell, Vera would have none to look to for help, none to defend her. She would be at the mercy of her persecutors! I think that thought appalled me even more than the thought that I might be tried for manslaughter or murder.

"Oh," I said at last to John, "it's some mistake. The police have made some grotesque blunder. You had better show them up, and I will talk to them."

No blunder had been made, and I knew it.

I must say that I was surprised at the officers' extreme courtesy. Seeing they were about to arrest me on suspicion of having caused a man's death, their politeness, their consideration for my feelings, had a touch of irony.

They waited while I had my bath and dressed. Then we all drove together to the police-station, chatting quite pleasantly on topics of passing interest. At the police-station my name and address and many other particulars, were taken down in writing. With the utmost gravity a pompous inspector asked me "what birthmarks I possessed, if any," and various other questions ending with "if any." I wondered whether, before he had done, he would ask me my sex—if any.

Nearly a month dragged on—days of anxiety, which seemed years, and I had had no word from Vera!

I shall never forget that trial—never.

My opinion of legal procedure, never high, sank to zero before the trial at the London Sessions ended. The absurdity of some of the questions asked by counsel; the impossible inferences drawn from quite ordinary occurrences;

the endless repetitions of the same questions, but in different sets of words; the verbal quibbling and juggling; the transposing of statements made in evidence and conveying a meaning obvious to the lowest intelligence; the pathos indulged in when the old man's end came to be described; the judge's weak attempts at being witty; the red-tapeism; the unpardonable waste of time—and of public money. No, I shall never forget those days.

It lasted from Monday till Thursday, and during those four days I spent eleven hours in the witness-box. Ah! what a tragic farce. I received anonymous letters of encouragement, and, of course, some offensive letters. I even received a proposal of marriage from a forward minx, who admitted that though still at school, in Blackheath, she had "read every word of the trial," that she "kept a dear portrait" of me, cut out of the *Daily Mirror*, under her pillow at night. I felt I must indeed have reached the depths of ignominy when my hand was sought in matrimony by an emotional Blackheath flapper. A pretty flapper, I admit. She sent me five cabinet portraits of herself, in addition to a miniature of herself as a baby. Phew! What are our young people coming to?

Well, in the end I was acquitted, and told that I might leave the Court without a stain upon my character.

Certainly that was in a sense gratifying. In the face of acrobatic verbal feats Counsel representing the Director of Public Prosecutions had indulged in during the trial, I felt that anything might have happened, and was fully prepared to be branded a felon for life. The drug, the jury decided, had been administered without any intention whatever to do more than send the old man to sleep for an hour or so, and an analysis of the tea left in the cup proved beyond a doubt, that this tea could not possibly have caused death, which had been due to heart-failure. I had been traced, it seemed, by my gloves and umbrella left in the old man's room. Other details—long-winded ones—I need not describe.

The problem now was, what to do next. My name, Richard Ashton, had become a sort of butt. Everybody knew it, had seen it in print twenty times during the past week. Mentioned by the comedian in a music-hall, it at once created laughter. I laughed myself—not uproariously, I admit—when a comedian at the Alhambra compared me to an albatross, thereby causing the entire audience to shake with merriment, and a stranger to turn to me with the remark—

"Richard Ashton! What a Nut, eh?"

Now the vulgar term "Nut" was in its infancy then, and new to me. I pawed the air in a vain endeavour to grasp the point of comparing me first to an albatross, and then to a nut. Nuts don't grow on ash trees, or I might have thought the "ash" of "Ashton" bore some kind of relationship to a nut. Finally I gave it up, convinced that I must be deficient in a sense of humour.

Meanwhile, my beloved had disappeared. To my chagrin I ascertained at the hotel at Hampstead that a man had called on the day following my arrest, and that she had gone away with him, taking all her luggage.

A description of the man failed to help me to identify him. From it I decided, however, that it was not Sir Charles who had called for Vera, nor yet the mysterious Smithson. My natural inference, therefore, was that the fellow Paulton had discovered her hiding-place, and compelled her to go away with him.

I tried hard to put into practice my theory that it is useless to worry about anything, and for some days I remained passive, watching, however, the advertisement columns in the principal daily newspapers, for during our evening at the hotel, Vera had incidentally remarked that she had, while at Brighton, advertised for a bracelet she had lost, and by that means recovered it. I advertised for news of her. But there was no response.

On the Sunday, having nothing particular to do, I looked in during the afternoon at one of my usual haunts, Tattersall's sale yard. I thought it probable I should there run across somebody or other I knew, and I was not mistaken. At the entrance I overtook a little man whose figure I could not mistake. The little sporting parson from a village outside Oakham was a great friend of mine, and he had told me that, whenever in town for a week-end he invariably went to Tattersall's on the Sunday afternoon to see what horses were to be sold there next day.

"Not that I can afford to buy a horse, oh dear no!" I remembered him saying to me in the drawing-room at Houghton. "You know what parson's families are. Mine is no exception to the rule!"

I had upbraided him for his lack of forethought, and he had chuckled, adding seriously that in his opinion the falling birth rate spelt the downfall of the Nation, a point upon which I had differed from him more than once.

"Hullo, Rowan!" I exclaimed, as I overtook him, and quietly slipped my arm into his from behind, making him start. "I see you spoke the truth that day."

He was frankly delighted to see me. I knew he would be, for he is one of the few Rutlanders I have met who are wholly devoid of what some Americans term "frills." I believe that if I were in rags and carrying a sandwich-board and I met little Rowan in the streets of London to-morrow, he would come up to me and grasp me by the hand. There are not many men of whom one can say that. I don't suppose more than ten per cent. of my acquaintances, if as many, would look at me again if next week I became a pauper.

"What truth, and when?" he asked, in answer to my remark.

"Don't you remember telling me," I said, "I believe it was the last time we hunted together, that when in London you always do two things? You said: 'I always attend service on Sunday morning, and Tattersall's on Sunday afternoon.' How is the old cob?"

"Getting old, Dick, getting old, like his master," Rowan said with a touch of pathos. "I hear the Hunt talk of buying me another mount. It is good of them; very good. I am not supposed to know, of course."

"And so you have come to find something up to your weight, eh?" I went on. He does not, I suppose, ride more than eight stone twelve in his hunting kit. He is the wiriest little man I have ever seen.

"No," he answered. "I have come to have a last look at Sir Charles Thorold's stud. It comes under the hammer to-morrow, as, of course, you know."

"Thorold's horses to be sold!" I exclaimed. "I had no idea. Then he has said good-bye to Rutland for good and all. I am sorry."

"So am I, very. He is a man I have always liked. Naturally his name is in rather bad odour in the county just at present, but that does not in the least affect my own regard for him."

"It wouldn't," I said to him. "You are not that sort, Rowan. It is a pity there are not more like you about."

He changed the subject by asking if I had seen Sir Charles and Lady Thorold lately.

"I have not seen Lady Thorold since the Houghton affair," I answered. "I have seen Sir Charles, but not to speak to."

I recollected how I had caught a glimpse of him in that house in Belgrave Street.

"You have heard the latest about Miss Thorold, of course?" he said, as we passed into the Yard, which at this hour—about four o'clock—was crowded with well-dressed men and women.

"The latest? What do you mean?"

"Dear me," he exclaimed, smiling. "Why, we country cousins know more than you men about town after all, sometimes. She's at Monte Carlo."

"At Monte? Vera Thorold!"

"Yes."

"What is she doing there? Who is with her?"

"I don't know who's with her, or if any one is with her. She is pretty independent, as you know, and well able to take care of herself—a typical twentieth century girl."

"But who told you she was at Monte?"

"Several people. Ah! there's Lord Logan! He'll tell us. He was speaking of her yesterday. He returned from the Riviera only a couple of days ago."

Chapter Twelve.

Gossip from the Sunshine.

"Oh, yes, that's right enough," Lord Logan said, when we questioned him. "I saw her the night before I left. She was playing trente-et-quarante—and winning a bit, too, by Gad!"

He was an ordinary type of the modern young peer—well-set-up, unemotional, faultlessly groomed. He produced a gold cigarette case as he spoke, and held it out to me. I noticed that the cigarettes it contained bore his coat of arms.

"These cigarettes are not likely to be stolen from you," I said lightly, indicating the coat of arms.

He smiled.

"You are right. I was the first to start the fashion—get 'em from Cairo every week—and now everybody's doin' it, haw, haw! I've got my cartridges done the same way. At some places where one shoots the beater fellers rob one right and left—the devils. I said to one of my hosts the other day, I said: 'Your cartridge carriers are a lot of bally rogues.' 'What do you mean?' he asked, bristlin' up like a well-bred bull-dog. 'Well,' I said, 'you make 'em all turn out their pockets, and you'll see,' I said. And he did!"

"And what was in them?"

"In them? Damme, what wasn't in them? My dear feller, every beater who had carried cartridges had a dozen or two cartridges in his pockets then—it's a fact. And we'd done shootin', and the beaters were goin' home, so they couldn't pretend they were just carryin' the bally cartridges in their pockets to have 'em handy. But there wasn't a cartridge of mine missing among the lot. They knew only too well they wouldn't be able to sell to the local ironmonger cartridges with a coat of arms on 'em—eh what? And that's why I now have my cigarettes tattooed in the same way. I believe my servants used to rob them by the hundred. They don't now, except perhaps a handful to smoke themselves, and of course that's only natural. What was it you were askin' me just now? Ah, yes, about Vera Thorold. She seems to be a flyer."

"Did you speak to her?"

"Oh, yes, I talked to her right enough. She did look well. Simply lovely. White cloth frock, you know. She's all alone at Monte, stayin' at the *Anglais*."

"Did she say how long she'd be there?"

"No. I didn't ask her. She was winnin' the night I saw her. I never saw such devil's luck—never. I lost over a thousand on the week, so I thought it time to pay my hotel bill—what?"

The three of us made the tour of Tattersall's together, admiring, criticising, fault-finding. Among Thorold's horses was the mare I had ridden on that last day I had been at Houghton. What a long time ago that seemed! I felt tempted to make a bid for her next day, she had carried me so well.

Then I thought again of my well-beloved. What an extraordinary girl she was! Ah! how I loved her. Why had she not told me that she meant to go to the Riviera? Why—

An idea flashed in upon me. I was getting bored with the mad hurry of London. This would be a good excuse for running out to the Côte d'Azur. Indeed, my chief reason for remaining in town had been that I believed Vera to be there still, either in hiding for some reason of her own, or, what I had thought far more likely, forced against her will by that blackguard Paulton to remain in concealment and keep me in ignorance of her whereabouts.

Instead of that she was "on her own"—how I hate that slang phrase—at Monte Carlo 'winnin' a fortune,' as Lord Logan had put it.

"A strange world, my masters!" Never were truer words spoken. The longer I live the more I realise its strangeness. When I arrived at Monte Carlo by the day rapide from Paris, rain was pelting down in torrents, and a fierce storm was raging. Wind shrieked along the streets. Out at sea, lightning flashed in the bay, while the thunder rattled like artillery fire. I was glad to find myself in the warm, brilliantly-lit *Hotel de Paris*, and when, after dinner, I strolled into the fumoir, it was so crowded that I had difficulty in finding any place to sit.

Among the group of men close to whom I presently found myself, conversation had turned upon the pigeon-shooting at Monte. From their remarks I gathered that an important event had been decided that day, the Prix de—I forget what, but the prize appeared to be a much coveted cup, with a considerable sum in added money. This had been won, it seemed, by a Belgian Count, who had killed twenty-seven pigeons without a miss.

"*Mais c'est épatant—vraiment épatant!*" declared an excitable little Frenchman, as he pulled forward his chair. He went on to explain, with great volubility and much gesticulation, the difficulties that some of the shots had presented. This Frenchman, I gathered further, had backed the Belgian Count every time from his first shot to the last, and had in consequence won a lot of money.

Time was when trap-shooting appealed to me. I have shot pigeons at Monte, at Ostend, and here in England at Hurlingham at the Gun Club, also at Hendon, but it has always struck me as being a cold-blooded form of amusement—its warmest supporters can hardly call it sport. Not that there is more cruelty connected with pigeon-shooting than with game-shooting, as some would have us believe. Indeed, I have always contended that trap-shooting is less cruel than game-shooting, for pigeon-shooters are one and all first-rate shots—if they were not they would lose heavily and soon give up the game—with the result that the greater proportion of the birds shot at are killed outright, a thing that cannot be said of game, where one's tailor sometimes takes out a licence.

But why is it, I wonder, that pigeon-shooters, considered collectively, are such dreadful-looking men? I have often wondered, and I am by no means the only man who has noticed this feature of pigeon-shooters. Glancing carelessly at the crowd seated near me now, it struck me forcibly that I had rarely set eyes on such a dissipated-looking set. Men of middle age, most of them, obese, fat-faced, with puffy eyes and sagging skin, they looked capable of any villainy, and might well have been addicted to every known vice.

One man in particular arrested my attention. His age was difficult to place. Lying, rather than sitting, back in a softly-padded leather chair, with crossed legs, and with one arm hanging loosely over the arm of the chair, he talked in a singularly ugly voice between his yellow teeth, which clenched a long cigar stuck in the corner of his mouth.

"Another twist, and he would have cleared the boundary," he was saying to his companion, a good-looking English lad of five-or-six-and-twenty. "The second barrel cut him to pieces; it's extraordinary what a lot of shot a blue-rock can carry away. How did you come out on the day?"

"Badly—shocking," answered the young man. "I backed the guns to start with, and you know how badly the whole lot of you shot. Then I started backing the bird, and you began to kill every time. My luck was out to-day—dead out."

I saw his friend smile.

"Dago was the one lucky man this afternoon, I should say," the first speaker remarked presently. "But there—he's always lucky."

Instantly my interest was aroused. "Dago!" Could it be—surely—?

"Yes, he's lucky enough," the other answered. Then, after a pause he added: "That's a man I can't stand."

"Can't stand? Why?"

"Oh, I don't know. The fellow gets on my nerves. How does he live? Have you any idea?"

"You mean, what is his source of income? I'm sure I can't tell you. But for that matter, how do half the men we meet here at Monte manage to live? It would not be well to ask. They have money, and that is the main thing. All we require is to transfer to our own pockets as much of it as we can."

The young man looked at him thoughtfully for some moments, then said—

"Yes, I suppose so."

The tone in which he spoke was ironical, but his companion didn't notice it.

"Do you know Paulton well?" the elder man asked himself.

"As well as I care to. Why do you ask?"

"Only just out of curiosity. Many people form an unfavourable impression of him when they meet him first, and afterwards they come to like him."

"That's the reverse of my case," answered the young man quickly. "The first time I met him I rather liked him, I remember. But after I had met him several times—well, I changed about him. He may be all right! I dare say he is. I suppose our personalities are not akin, as I have heard some one put it."

"He's a fine shot."

"You are right. He is. I thought he would win the cup to-day."

"The bird that knocked him out was badly hit. If he had killed it, he would have won second money."

The young Englishman lay back, stretched himself, and yawned. "I'm getting fed up with this place," he said at last. "I shall get back to England in a day or two. How long shall you remain here?"

"It depends—partly on Dago. We're running a sort of syndicate together, you know—or probably you don't know. He has to see one or two men here about it before we leave."

"What sort of syndicate?"

"I am afraid I'm not at liberty to tell you—yet. I can tell you this—though, we have a lady interested in it, a very pretty girl. That ought to appeal to you," and he laughed.

"Have I seen her?" the young man asked, looking at him curiously.

His companion pondered. Then suddenly he exclaimed—

"Why, yes—of course you have. She was playing trente-et-quarante the other night, and nothing could stop her winning. She won a maximum and went on and on, simply raking in the money. You and I were there together. I am sure you must remember."

"*That* girl!"

The tone in which he uttered these words surprised me. Could it be Vera of whom they had been speaking? According to Lord Logan she had won heavily at trente-et-quarante. And if so, who was this man, this partner and friend of Dago Paulton's? And what could the secret syndicate be in which both were interested?

I had my back to the door, and the middle-aged man who spoke between his teeth and was lying back in the lounge chair was almost facing me. Suddenly, a look of recognition came into his eyes—he had seen some one behind me enter, whom he knew.

"Ah, here is good old Dago," he exclaimed. He held up his hand and signalled to him.

I had fitted a cigarette into my holder, struck a match, and lit up slowly, while I composed my thoughts. Now I half-turned to gaze upon this man of whom I had heard so much, and was now to see for the first time.

Chapter Thirteen.

In the Web.

I held my breath.

I should have recognised him at once from the panel portrait, though he looked some years older than when that photograph had been taken.

Of medium height, and rather broadly built, he had all the appearance of a gentleman. His hair was very short, with dark grey, rather deep-set eyes, and thick dark eyebrows. The hair was parted in the middle, and plastered down, but he was not in evening clothes, as were the men to whose conversation I had been listening.

He shook hands cordially with his friend, nodded to the good-looking young man, and called to the waiter to bring him a chair, those near by being all occupied. While waiting for the chair to be brought, he suddenly caught sight of me, evidently in recognition, for he turned quickly and spoke in a low tone to his friend, who at once glanced in my direction.

All this I "felt" rather than saw, for I was not looking directly at the two men.

Where had Paulton seen me before? That was the first thought that occurred to me, and of course I could not answer it. I had no recollection of having ever seen him previously. Suddenly, he crossed over to me.

"Mr Richard Ashton, I think?" he said in a genial tone, and with a smile.

"Yes," I answered rather stiffly, none too pleased at his addressing me. I certainly had no wish to know him.

"My name's Paulton," he said, ignoring my coldness. "I've seen you before. You were pointed out to me one night at the Savoy. I want to introduce my friend. Henderson, let me present you to Mr Richard Ashton. Mr Ashton—Mr Henderson."

It was done before I could say anything—before I could avoid it. There was nothing for it, therefore, but to pretend to appear pleased.

He asked me what I would drink, and I had to say something—though I hated drinking with the fellow. Put yourself in my place—drinking with a man who had tried in cold blood to kill me, and who had shot an innocent man dead! I felt it had been weak of me not to ignore his greeting and meet his look of recognition with a stony stare. But regret for a mistake was useless now. I had made a false step when I spoke to him, and I couldn't suddenly, apparently for no reason, turn my back upon him.

A sudden terrific gust of wind shook the heavy windows, and a sheet of rain splashed against the panes like a great wave, distracting, for the moment, every one's attention. A storm on the Riviera is always heavy and blustering.

"I have just come in," Paulton said. "In all my life I don't recollect such an awful storm as this, except once in the Jura, when I was out boar-shooting. How fortunate it didn't start while the pigeon-shooting was on to-day."

He turned to me suddenly.

"By the way, Ashton," he said familiarly, "we have a mutual friend, I think."

"Indeed?" I answered drily. "Who is that?"

"Sir Charles Thorold's daughter, Miss Vera."

I was astonished at this effrontery—so astounded that my surprise outweighed my feeling of indignation at the tone of familiarity in which he spoke of Vera. He might have been referring to some barmaid we both knew.

I think he detected my annoyance, but he said nothing. After a pause I replied, keeping myself in check—

"Is Miss Thorold a friend of yours?"

"A friend of mine? Rather. I should say so!"

He glanced across at Henderson, and they both smiled significantly. This was intolerable.

"I do know Miss Thorold," I remarked, emphasising the "Miss Thorold," "but I don't remember that she has ever mentioned your name to me."

"No, probably she wouldn't mention it. Vera is discreet, if she is nothing else."

The impertinence of this reply was so obvious, so pointed, that I knew it must have been intentional.

"Really, I don't follow you," I said icily. "What, pray, has Miss Thorold to say to you, and what have you to say to her?"

"Oh, a very great deal, I can assure you."

"Indeed? How intensely interesting!"

"It is, very. Her flight from Houghton that night must have astonished you."

I could bear the fellow's company no longer. Emptying my tumbler, I rose with deliberation, and, excusing myself with frigid politeness, strode out of the fumoir.

In the vestibule I met the good-looking young Englishman. He had left the room soon after Paulton had entered. Now he came up and spoke to me.

"I hope you'll forgive my addressing you," he said in well-bred accents, raising his hat, "but I heard your name mentioned when Paulton introduced Henderson to you. May I ask if you are *the* Mr Richard Ashton?"

"It depends what you mean by 'the' Richard Ashton," I answered. This young man attracted me; he had done so from the first.

"Do you happen to live in King Street, St. James's?" he inquired abruptly.

"Yes, I do."

"Then you're the man I have for weeks past been wanting to meet. I believe you know Miss Thorold—Miss Vera Thorold."

"I do."

"She wants particularly to see you."

"How do you know that?"

"Because she told me, or rather a friend of hers—to whom I am engaged to be married—did. They are together at the *Alexandra Hotel*, in Mentone. My friend is staying there with an aunt of mine."

"Surely if Miss Thorold wished to meet me she could have written to me, or telegraphed," I said rather frigidly.

"No. I think I ought to tell you that the man who introduced himself to you some minutes ago—the man Dago Paulton—has entire control over her—she goes in fear of him! She did not dare write to you, or even send you a wire. She knew that if she did he would find out. The lady to whom I am engaged told me this some days ago, and told me a great deal about you that had been told to her by Miss Thorold."

"Do you mind telling me your name?" I said, looking at him squarely.

"Faulkner—Frank Faulkner. Paulton is a man of whom you ought to be very careful. He is really a scoundrel, that I don't mind telling you. I have just been told by a man who really knows, that he has forced Miss Thorold to take an active interest in a rascally scheme of some kind that he and Henderson have devised. I am told by my lady friend—her name is Gladys Deroxe—that Miss Thorold tried her utmost to have nothing to do with it, but Paulton threatened to reveal something he knows concerning her father, so in the end she consented. Paulton has no longer a card for the Rooms; he was shut out last year for some reason, and he has lately been compelling Miss Thorold to go and play there in his place. Her luck at trente-et-quarante has been phenomenal, but all the money she has won he has of course at once taken from her, she is his factotum. I am very glad for her sake that you have come out. I suppose it was by accident you came? You didn't expect to find her here—eh?"

"On the contrary," I said, "I chanced to hear only last Sunday that Miss Thorold was staying on the Riviera—so I decided to come over at once," I said.

"She knows that you are here, you know."

"She knows? Why, who on earth can have told her?"

"I have just been telephoning to Miss Deroxe over at the *Bristol* at Beaulieu. Miss Thorold is there with her. I told them that a man named Ashton was here, and I described your appearance. Miss Thorold said at once it must be you. Unfortunately she leaves to-night for Paris, and Miss Deroxe goes with her."

"But why is she going to Paris?" I exclaimed eagerly.

"Who? Miss Thorold? She's acting on Paulton's orders. Her visit has some mysterious bearing upon the scheme I have just spoken about."

The door of the fumoir opened at that moment, and Paulton and Henderson came out into the vestibule. At once they must have seen Faulkner and myself conversing, and for an instant a look of anger flashed into Paulton's eyes. The expression subsided quickly, and he and Henderson approached smiling calmly.

"I'm prepared to bet that I know what you two were talking about," Paulton said lightly, addressing Faulkner. "You were talking of Vera. Ah! Am I wrong? No, I see I'm not. You have told our friend Ashton that she goes to Paris to-night. Well, you are mistaken. Information has reached me that there has been a landslip on the line beyond Beaulieu, and it is blocked in consequence."

Then he turned to me.

"Would you like to come over to Beaulieu, Ashton?" he said, as though making some quite ordinary request. "My car will be here presently. I can take you too, Faulkner, if you wish to see Miss Deroxe. I am going straight to the *Bristol*."

I was about to refuse, when Faulkner spoke.

"I should like to go, and Mr Ashton will of course come."

"Good. My car should be here in a quarter of an hour."

He strolled over to the bureau, and I heard him inquire for letters. There were several. He took them from the gold-laced porter, sank on to a settee, and began to tear them open.

"Why did you accept his offer?" I inquired of Faulkner, in an undertone, as I lit a cigarette.

"Never mind," he answered quickly. "I know what I'm doing. Leave everything to me now." At that moment the large glazed double doors leading into the Place in front of the Casino revolved slowly and a tall, imposing-looking woman of thirty-five or so, in rich black furs, which had all the appearance of being valuable, sailed in, followed by her maid carrying a small bag. Paulton, glancing up from his letters, noticed her, and at once sprang to his feet.

"Ah, Baronne, how pleasant to meet you again!" he exclaimed, as he approached her. "I expected you here sooner."

"I should have been here an hour ago," she exclaimed, "but the train was delayed. This storm is awful!"

She had a rich, deep contralto voice, one of those speaking voices that at once arouse interest and curiosity. It aroused interest now, for the guests seated in the hall simultaneously interrupted their conversation in order to look at the new arrival, so striking was her appearance.

"I went to the station quite a while ago," Paulton said. "They told me the train could not arrive."

"It has not arrived yet, I believe," she answered. "I got off at a wayside station, drove the two miles into Beaulieu, and then hired the car which has just brought me on here."

She was indeed a handsome woman, obviously a woman of singular personality. Exceedingly dark, with great coils of blue-black hair that her travelling-veil only partly concealed, she was very handsome still. When I had watched her for nearly a minute, wondering whom she might be, my gaze unconsciously drifted to the quietly-dressed maid who stood respectfully and demurely a few feet behind her mistress, bearing a large leather dressing-case in her hand. Her appearance somehow seemed familiar. Suddenly she turned her face rather more towards me, and I recognised her at once.

It was Judith, the French girl who had been Lady Thorold's maid. Her beady little black eyes rested on me for an instant, then were quietly lowered. But instinctively I knew that in that single, swift glance she had recognised me—and I certainly held her in suspicion.

"The rooms have been retained for you Baronne," I heard Paulton say, "the rooms you had last year. Shall I order supper?"

"Certainly. Please do," the deep voice answered. "Tell Gustave to send it to my rooms in a quarter of an hour. Ma foi! I am famished."

For the first time I noticed that she spoke with a foreign accent. But it was not very marked.

"Then I shall see you later," Paulton said, as the new arrival moved towards the lift. "*À tantôt*, Baronne."

"*À bientôt.*"

Paulton bent over her hand, and when the doors of the lift had shut he came across to us.

"You'd better get into your coats," he said. "My car is just coming round!"

"Who is the lady?" Faulkner asked carelessly.

"Who?" Paulton exclaimed. "You don't mean to say you don't know Baronne de Coudron? I thought everybody in Monte knew the Baronne—by sight. She's one of my best friends."

As the big grey Rolls-Royce sped through the darkness, the storm still raged. None of us spoke. Three glowing cigars alone indicated our whereabouts.

Whether or not it was the stiff brandy-and-soda I had had in the smoking-room, I know not, but I suddenly realised that I was becoming curiously drowsy. I tried to keep awake. My eyelids felt like lead. They were smarting, too. Presently I was aware that something glowing red had fallen to the ground. Afterwards I came to know it had been Faulkner's cigar.

I do not know what happened immediately afterwards. My mind suddenly became a complete blank.

At last, hours afterwards, I suppose, I slowly struggled back to consciousness.

Where was I?

The room, and all in it, was strange to me. All was utterly unfamiliar. My head ached very badly. My back and limbs were stiff. I got off the sofa where I had lain asleep, scrambled to my feet, and looked about me. At once I saw Faulkner. He was asleep still, in a most uncomfortable attitude, in a big leather armchair. His mouth was wide open.

A glance out of the window showed me that the house we were in was in the open country. Already it was broad daylight, and a perfect calm had succeeded the storm of the previous night. But had it been the previous night? I supposed so. Signs of the storm were still visible everywhere—trees blown down and lying on their sides, branches and great limbs lying about. The country all around was densely wooded. Look in what direction I would, only trees, grass fields and mountains were visible. There was not a house in sight; not a cottage; not a hut.

I went over to Faulkner, and shook him roughly. He was still sleeping soundly, and it took me some minutes to arouse him into consciousness.

His first observation when at last fully awake, was characteristic of the young man—

"Where, in Heaven's name, am I?"

Chapter Fourteen.

The Perfume.

I dashed across to the door. It was locked. "Now tell me, what do you make of it?" Faulkner asked, when he had looked about the unfamiliar room and stared blankly out of the window.

"The solution seems pretty obvious," I said. "We've been drugged, or in some way made unconscious last night in Paulton's car, and driven here. I distinctly remember trying to keep awake. You gave me that cigar I smoked. Was it one of your own?"

He paused, then said—

"Now I come to think of it, Ashton, I remember noticing I had three cigars in the case I left in the pocket of my overcoat when I hung it in the cloakroom. There were only two when I pulled the case out in the car. I wondered then if the cloakroom attendant had helped himself. Paulton was the first to light up, you may remember, and he offered us cigars, whereupon I said I had some, and I gave you one of mine—one of the two. It struck me that my cigar had rather a peculiar flavour, but after a while it got all right. I believe those weeds must have been slipped into my case by Paulton and my own cigars removed. The ones we smoked last night were drugged, that I will swear."

I pulled out my watch.

"What time do you make it?" I asked. "My watch has stopped."

He produced his own and glanced at it.

"So has mine," he said. "It stopped at five minutes to four."

We both sat in silence for some moments. Obviously there was nothing to be done but to wait for somebody to come. The door was locked, there was no bell in the room, and the room was on an upper floor.

Over an hour must have passed, and we had endeavoured to take our bearings.

From what we could see of the place from the high up window, it was a huge rambling old château with round turrets, and slated roofs, overlooking a large sloping park in the midst of picturesque mountains, many of which were still tipped with snow. The situation was perfect, but it was in a remote, lonely spot, without another house in sight.

In the front was a long double colonnade with a terrace which commanded a fine vista down the valley. The style was that of Louis XV, as indeed was the furniture of the room, and there were several old paintings and works of art in the apartment.

It was a huge grim place, which seemed to be half a prison, half a fortress—a place wherein dwelt the ghosts of a glorious long-forgotten past. There was an air of neglect and decay about its time-mellowed court-yard, some of the walls of which were half-hidden by ivy. One of the round towers indeed was roofless, while what had once been an Italian flower-bed was now but a wilderness of weeds.

Outside the sun shone brightly, and, from its position, we concluded the hour must be nearly noon. Then, all at once we simultaneously caught the sound of footsteps. Some one was coming very softly apparently, along a carpeted passage outside the door. I went across to the sofa, lay down, and pretended to be asleep, Faulkner following my example, lying back in the big chair. At the door the footsteps stopped. There was a pause. Then a key was inserted into the lock almost noiselessly, the lock clicked, the handle turned, and the door was pushed open a little way.

Somebody bent over me. I breathed heavily, in pretence of sleep. The footsteps moved away, and, as I parted my eyelids slightly, I saw a woman—quite a young girl. She had her back to me and was bending over Faulkner apparently to ascertain if he too, were asleep. Acting upon a sudden impulse I sprang from the sofa, ran to the door, slammed it, and stood with my back to it.

To my surprise the girl looked at me quite calmly.

"I knew you would do that m'sieur," she said, and her voice, though she spoke with a marked French accent, was very pleasant. "Did you think that I supposed you both were asleep? Ah, non, your friend here is wide awake, though he too keeps his eyes shut and his mouth open."

The girl was quite pretty, about eighteen I judged, refined in appearance, with large, innocent brown eyes, dark eyelashes and eyebrows, and auburn hair that turned to shining gold as the sun's rays, entering at the window, touched it.

As she stopped speaking, Faulkner opened his eyes, sat up, and stared at her with undisguised admiration. Then, as the absurdity of the situation struck us, we both laughed.

"Whoever you are," I said, trying to speak seriously, though, under the circumstances, and with a pretty girl staring into my face, with an expression in her eyes that was partly of amusement and partly mockery, I found it hard to do so. "Whoever you are, I should really like an explanation."

"Explanation of what?"

"I want to know why we have been brought here—what place this is, and who had the cool impertinence to lock us in here."

"Oh, *I* had the cool impertinence to lock you in," she answered, smiling.

"You! And who are you? And whose house is this?"

"This is the Château d'Uzerche. It belongs to the Baronne de Coudron. I am the Baronne's niece."

"The Château d'Uzerche—eh?"

I could not for the moment, think of anything else to say. The girl spoke quite naturally, as though nothing unusual had occurred.

"I am going to bring your déjeuner in a minute," she said, drawing down the blinds to keep out the sun. "Will you both give me your word you won't leave this room if I leave the door unlocked? Please do—for my sake."

She looked so captivating as she said this, her voice was so soft, and altogether she seemed so charming, that Faulkner at once answered that he had not the least desire to leave the room if she would promise to come back as quickly as possible, and to stay a little while.

"Then you will promise?" she asked, her big eyes set on his.

"How foolish! Why?" I asked, interrupting.

"Well," she replied. "If you will remain here I will bring you a visitor."

"A visitor?"

"Yes," she laughed. "Somebody you know."

"Who?"

"A great friend of yours."

I looked at her puzzled.

"A friend—man or woman?"

"Female," she assured us with a charming accent. "Your friend Mademoiselle Thorold."

"Vera!" I gasped. "Is she here?"

"Yes," was her reply. "She is here."

How well Vera knew my character when she told me that day I was "susceptible." I think I am dreadfully so. The look in those great brown eyes gazing into mine seemed to weaken my will until I had to answer almost sulkily—

"I suppose I must. Yes, I—well, I'll promise for the present anyhow," I said.

"Not to leave this room before my return?" she said.

"Not to leave this room before you return," I repeated.

Then she left us, and we sat looking at each other like a pair of fools.

"Well," Faulkner said. "If you can be rude to a pretty girl like that, Ashton, I can't, and I don't intend to be. Besides, if Vera is here, Gladys may be here also!"

"I thought you said you are engaged to be married?"

"I did. And I am. But I don't see why, for that reason, you need call me a fool for being ordinarily polite to another woman, or to any woman, especially if we are to meet Vera."

"You quite mistake my meaning," I said. "I say we are a pair of fools—I am more to blame perhaps than you—for being coerced by a chit of a girl into promising to stay here, as though we were a pair of schoolboys put 'on their honour.' It is downright silly, to say the least. Yet we must not break our *parole*—eh?"

I liked Faulkner. His spirit, and his way of saying what he thought amused me. One meets so few men nowadays with pluck enough to say what they really think and mean.

The young girl, whose name was Violet—Violet de Coudron—spread the white cloth, laid the table, and herself brought in our déjeuner. What position did she occupy in the house, we both wondered. Surely there must be servants, and yet... where was Vera?

"You have to stay here until to-morrow," she said, when we had begun our meal—the cooking was excellent, and the wine was above reproach.

"And, until then, you are under my supervision. Those are my orders."

"Your orders, received from whom—eh?" I asked.

"Mademoiselle Thorold wishes it."

"Were we brought here yesterday, or when?" Faulkner asked presently.

"About two o'clock this morning."

"And what was this grim joke?"

"That I may not tell you, m'sieur," she replied. "Indeed, I couldn't tell you—for I don't know. Miss Thorold knows."

"Who lives here usually?" I asked. "The Baronne?"

"She is rarely here. But that is enough. I cannot answer more questions. Is there anything else that I can get you?"

Nothing else we needed, except tobacco, and she brought us that. Very good tobacco it was, too.

Wearily the day passed, for though the room we were in was well-furnished, there were few books in it. We could, of course, have gone out of the room, out of the house probably, but our pretty little wardress had placed us on *parole*.

Whether or not the house was occupied, even whether there were servants in it, we could not tell. And the matter did not interest us much. What we should have liked to know was, why we had been brought there, still more, how Vera Thorold and Gladys Deroxe were faring in our absence. During the past weeks my life seemed to have been made up of a series of mysteries, each more puzzling than the last. I was distracted.

During the afternoon, while sitting together, very dejected, we suddenly caught the faint sound of a female voice singing.

Both of us listened. It was Vera's voice, a sweet contralto, and she was singing, as though to herself, Verlaine's "Manoline," that sweet harmonious song—

> "Les donneurs de sérénades,
> Et les belles écouteuses,
> Échangent des propos fades
> Sous les ramures chanteuses.
>
> "C'est Tircis et c'est Aminte
> Et c'est l'éternel Clitandre
> Et c'est Damis qui pour mainte cruelle
> Fait maint vers tendre."

The girl brought us tea presently, and, late in the evening, a plain dinner. The room was lit by petrol-gas. Each time she stayed with us a little while, and we were glad to have her company. She was, however, exceedingly discreet, refusing to make any statement which might throw light upon the reason of our confinement.

How strange it all was. Vera did not appear. We laughed at our own weakness and our own chivalry.

She showed us the bedroom where we were to sleep. Beautifully and expensively-furnished, it had two comfortable-looking beds, while a log-fire burnt cheerily in the grate—for the evening after the sunshine was singularly chilly in the mountains.

"If Vera does not come by mid-day to-morrow," Faulkner said, as we prepared to get into bed, "I shall break my *parole* and set out to discover where she is. Our pretty friend is all very well, but my patience is exhausted. I'm not in need of a rest cure just at present."

We had both been asleep, I suppose, for a couple of hours, when I suddenly awoke. The room was in total darkness, but somehow I "felt" the presence of some stranger in the room. At that instant it flashed in upon me that we had left the door unlocked. Straining my ears to catch the least sound, I held my breath.

Suddenly a noise came to me, not from the room, but from somewhere in the house. It was a cry—A cry for help! Sitting bolt upright in the bed, I remained motionless, listening intently. I heard it again. It was a woman's cry—but this time fainter—

"Help! *Help!*" sounded in a long drawn-out gasp—a gasp of despair.

Something moved in the darkness. Again I "felt," rather than heard it. My mouth grew dry, and fear, a deadly fear of the unknown, possessed me.

"Who is there?" I called out loudly.

There was no answer, but the sound of my voice gave me courage. I stretched my arm out in the darkness, meaning to reach over to Faulkner's bed and prod him into wakefulness, when by chance I touched something alive.

Instantly a cold, damp hand gripped my own, holding it like a vice, and a moment later I was flung down on my back on the bed, and held there firmly by a silent, unseen foe.

In vain I struggled to get free, but the speechless, invisible Thing pressing me down in the darkness, kept me pinned to the bed! I was about to cry out, when a third hand closed about my throat, preventing me. It was a soft hand—a woman's hand. Also, as it gripped me, a faint perfume struck my nostrils, a perfume familiar to me, curious, rich, pungent.

And then, almost as I stopped struggling, the room was suddenly flooded with light.

Chapter Fifteen.

Within an Ace.

Slowly I realised that Paulton was bending over me, holding me down.

The Baronne de Coudron, upon the opposite side of the bed, had her thin, strong sinewy hands upon my throat. Beside the gas-jet a yard or two away, Faulkner stood with his hand still holding the little chain he had pulled in order to turn on the light.

Nobody spoke.

The Baronne, removing her hands from me, stood upright, big and strong, gazing down upon me still. She wore an elaborate kimono made of some soft pink Eastern material. Paulton was in evening clothes, one shirt-cuff was turned back.

"You should have taken my advice, m'sieur," the Baronne said in her deep voice, addressing Dago Paulton. She spoke quite calmly.

Instead of answering, and without loosening hold, he half-turned, apparently undecided what to do, until his eyes rested upon Faulkner. Then suddenly, to my surprise, he released me. I got up.

"Faulkner, come here," he said sharply.

The young man—he was in the blue pyjamas he had found laid out upon the bed when Violet de Coudron had shown us into the bedroom—looked quietly at the speaker for a moment or two, then answered with the utmost sang-froid—

"I'm not your servant, hang you! Don't speak to me like that."

"You may not be my servant, but I now control your movements," Paulton retorted quickly. "Therefore you will please do what I order. I take it that you know that I brought you and Ashton over here."

"Naturally."

"Have you any idea why?"

"None."

"Then I will tell you. Listen."

He was standing beside the bed. The Baronne, near him, looked with interest at Faulkner and myself as we now stood together a yard or two away from them.

"For some months past," Paulton said, watching me with an unpleasant expression, "you have been on intimate terms with the Thorolds."

"Really," I answered, shortly, "I can't see what concern that is of yours. I have known the Thorolds intimately for a good many years. Perhaps you will tell me your reason for the extraordinary liberty you took last night in bringing us here. I consider it a gross impertinence."

"Impertinence!" he laughed. "Let me tell you both," he said, "that you have to thank this lady," he turned slightly to indicate the Baronne, "for being alive to-day. When I brought you here I intended that neither of you should ever again be heard of. Your disappearance would have made a stir, no doubt, but the stir would not have lasted; you would soon have been forgotten here. Dead men tell no tales. But the Baronne interfered."

"I'm sure we feel deeply grateful," I answered ironically. "One would think we were conspirators, or criminals, by the way you talk. So far as I'm aware, I never set eyes on you until last night in the *Hotel de Paris*."

"Quite likely," he replied, "but that is beside the point. You possess information you have no right to possess. You know the Thorolds' secret, and until your lips are closed I shall not feel safe." Ah! that remarkable secret again! What on earth could it be? That was the thought that flashed across my mind, but I merely answered—"You can't suppose I shall reveal it?"

He smiled coldly.

"Not reveal it, man, when you know what is at stake! You must think me very confiding if you suppose I shall trust your bare assurance. As I have said, I intended to—to—well, to close both your mouths."

"Why Faulkner's," I asked.

"Because he is to marry Gladys Deroxe, who is so friendly with Vera Thorold, who is to be my wife. Vera knows too much, and may have told her little friend what she knows. I mistrust Vera's friends—even her friends' friends. You understand?"

"At that rate," I answered, growing reckless, "you will need to 'remove' a good many people."

"That is possible. It is for that reason—"

"Oh, why talk so much!" the Baronne interrupted impatiently. "Tell him everything in a few words, and have done with it!"

"I will." He said fiercely, "You both stand in my way. I brought you here last night to get rid of you. I came into this room some minutes ago to carry out my plan. I was going to kill you both with an anaesthetic. Then the Baronne came in, threatening to wake you if I tried to do what I had said I should. I felt you touch me in the dark, I knew we had awakened you, and at once seized you—the Baronne held your throat to prevent your calling out. Then Faulkner sprang up and turned on the light and—"

He paused, listening. There had been another cry for help, barely audible even in the stillness of the night. He glanced at his companion. She too had heard it.

They looked meaningly at each other, but neither moved to leave the room. The cry had sounded so piteous that I should myself have rushed out to ascertain whence it came. Was it Vera's voice? Paulton was near the door, and to have passed him would have been impossible.

Was it my Vera? The thought held me in a frenzy.

"There is only one way," he went on, as though nothing had happened, "for you to regain your liberty. I should not offer even this, had not the Baronne persuaded me to against my better judgment."

"What is the way?"

"You must never attempt to see Vera again. And you, Faulkner, must write at once to Gladys Deroxe and break off your engagement. It is the only alternative. Do you both agree?"

Neither of us answered. The suggestion was a childlike one.

"Is there no other way?" I asked at last in order to gain time.

"None."

"Then I refuse absolutely," Faulkner exclaimed hotly.

"Your proposal is ridiculous," I declared with a grin.

Paulton turned furiously on the Baronne.

"I said what it would be!" he broke out with a curse. "Get out of my way!"

She had sprung in front of him, but he pushed her aside. Again she rushed forward to stop his doing something—we had not guessed what it was—and this time he struck her a blow in the face with his open hand, and with a cry she fell forward on to the bed.

Beside myself, I leapt forward, but Faulkner was nearer to him and I saw his fist fly out. I did not know then that Faulkner had won "friendly bouts" against professional light-weight boxers at the National Sporting Club. It was a stunning blow, Faulkner's fist hit him on the mouth, at what boxers call the "crucial moment," that is, just before the arm straightens. Paulton reeled backward, his lower lip rent almost to the chin.

His hand disappeared. Now it flashed out with a Browning pistol, but as the shot rang out the woman leapt to her feet and struck his arm away. An instant later Faulkner was behind him deftly twisting his left arm so that he bent backward with a scream of pain.

I had wrested the weapon from him ere he could shoot again, and as I helped Faulkner to hold him down I realised the man's colossal strength. Mad with fury, and with blood pouring from his mouth, he struggled to get free. But the twisted arm that Faulkner still clutched tightly by the wrist with both hands, kept him down. Suddenly he changed his tactics. He had wormed himself half round on the floor, his teeth closed tightly upon Faulkner's right shoulder.

"Twist his right arm—quick!" Faulkner shouted at me.

I did so, and the man lay flat upon his back, his two arms screwed so tightly that I marvelled they did not break.

The strange, warm smell that I had noticed in the room for the first time some minutes previously, and that had gradually grown stronger, was now so oppressive that it almost stifled us. Still holding down our man, we both glanced about the room to find out whence it came, and now we noticed that the atmosphere was foggy, or so it seemed. The Baronne was standing by us, staring down at Paulton, but not attempting in any way to help him. Her gaze was dull, almost vacant. She seemed stupefied.

An odd noise, as of distant roaring, sounded somewhere in the house. It was growing louder. All at once I saw the Baronne move quickly to the door. She listened for a moment, then turned the handle slowly.

As the door opened a little way, a cloud of dense, yellow smoke swept into the room, choking and nearly blinding us. She slammed the door and locked it.

"*Dieu!*" she gasped, pale as death.

And then, simultaneously, we knew the awful truth, that the château was on fire; that our only way of escape was made impassable by smoke.

Chapter Sixteen.

The Harvest of Fire.

In face of Death human antagonism becomes suddenly absorbed in the mad craving for Life.

The bitter hatred, the fearful rage, the furious struggle of the past few minutes were, in that instant, forgotten as though they had never been. Speechless with terror we gazed hopelessly at each other. Ah! I can see that picture still. Am I ever likely to forget it?

The Baronne, deathly white, stood there a handsome figure, trembling in her wonderfully embroidered pink kimono, her eyes fixed and starting as though madness were stealing into her brain. Paulton stood with his lips badly cut. Young Faulkner was erect and calm, with set teeth, blood spattered about his pyjamas, and an angry red wound showing at the spot where Paulton in his frenzy had bitten into his shoulder.

Truly, it was a weird and terrible scene. I stood aghast.

The fierce devouring roar in the house increased. It sounded like a furnace heard at night in the Black Country. Quickly the air grew thicker. Through the door, dark yellow, choking smoke percolated, then rolled upward in spirals that became merged in the general atmosphere.

We both slipped into our clothes hurriedly. Then Faulkner was the first to act.

Crossing quickly to the window, he pulled aside the curtains, thrust down the handle, and pushed open both frames. A red, quivering glow flickered in the blackness of the night, revealing for an instant the level meadow far below, the trees silhouetted upon it, the outlines of a distant wood.

Now he was kneeling on the broad window-sill of the long casement window, his body thrust far out. I saw him glance to right and left, then look down towards the earth. Slowly he drew back. Once more he stood amongst us.

"We are pretty high up," he said, without any sign of emotion. "Thirty feet I should say."

He looked about him. Then he went over to the beds, and pulled off all the clothes.

"Six blankets and six sheets—but I wouldn't trust the sheets, and the blankets are too short," he observed as though nothing unusual were happening.

A washstand, a couple of antique wardrobes, four chairs with high carved backs, a dressing-table and a smaller table, was all that the room contained besides the beds. He glanced up at the ceiling. It was solid. He tore up the carpet. Beneath it was a loose board, hinged. He lifted it by the ring. Smoke rolled up into his face, and he slammed the board down again, stamping his foot upon it. And at that instant the gas suddenly went out.

In the sky, the lurid light still rose and fell over the meadows and hills. The fierce roaring in the house grew louder. From a cover beyond the lawn came the echo of crackling wood and cracking timber, but nowhere was a human voice audible.

At this juncture, to my amazement, Faulkner calmly produced his cigarette case, lit a cigarette, topped it and offered me one. I took it without knowing what I did—I, who had so often pretended that in a moment of crisis I should never lose my head!

"What's to be done?" I gasped, beside myself. "Where is Vera?" I knew that in another moment I should be upon my knees, praying as I had only once in my life prayed before. It is, alas, only at such times that many of us think of our Maker and invoke His aid. In the ordinary course of life prayers weary so many of us and we feel we do not need them. I remember still, a typhoon off Japan, and how everybody prayed fervently. Yet when the seas subsided, and we felt safe once more, we all pretended we forgot how frightened we had been, and especially how we had implored forgiveness for our sins and promised never to sin again. We humans are, after all, but abject cowards.

"There is nothing to be done, that I can see," Faulkner answered. He glanced again at the beds, now naked of coverings, then up at the curtain-pole over the window. He pulled over the smaller table, climbed on to it, then proceeded, leisurely as it seemed to me, to examine the rings of the curtain-pole with the help of the bedroom candle he held above his head. Every second brought us nearer a terrible fate.

"These are good stout hooks," he said, puffing smoke out of his nose. "They ought to hold all right. What do you think, Ashton?"

"Oh, for the love of Heaven do something—*anything*!" I exclaimed, for already the room was stifling, and down the passage the fire could be heard crackling as it ate its way towards us. "I don't know what to think. I don't know what you mean, or what you ask me."

"Why," he answered, "we can easily get the steel cross-pieces off those bedsteads, and, hooked one to another with these stout brass curtain-hooks they will reach to the ground easily. The question is—how shall we be able to secure the top one, and, when it is secured, shall we be able to let ourselves down the steel bands without cutting our hands to pieces? These flat bedstead bands are very sharp, you know."

He remained fiddling with the hooks with one hand, while with the other he still held the candle above his head. The heat was becoming intolerable. Now we could hardly see across the room, and the smoke hurt our eyes.

All this had happened quickly, though in my dread the seconds seemed hours.

A wild cry in the room made us start. The Baronne had apparently gone suddenly mad. Dashing towards the door, she unlocked it and flung it wide open. An instant later she had disappeared—rushed out into the blinding smoke.

I ran at the door to slam it. As I did so I stumbled over something on the floor, and fell heavily.

I had stumbled over Paulton. In a paroxysm of terror he knelt there, motionless. He was praying! At any other time I should have felt nothing but unutterable contempt for him—a man I believed to be a murderer, driven through sheer mental torture to mumble prayers to his Creator whose name I had several times heard him blasphemously invoke. Now I felt only pity— intense pity. But I had no time to think. Clambering to my feet I managed to reach the door through the smoke that choked me, and to shut it securely. The Baronne de Coudron had, I knew, rushed to her death in her sudden access of madness—madness induced by terror.

Faulkner had removed all the hooks from which the heavy curtain-rings had hung. Now he was at work wrenching the steel bedstead binders from their sockets and hooking them together. Mechanically I helped him. And all the time I could hear Paulton, hidden in the darkness, beseeching the Almighty to save him from a terrible death.

Louder and louder grew the roar of the approaching fire, and with it the crackling of the woodwork and the falling of scorched walls. From afar came the sound of a mighty crash, the glare in the sky brightened, a thousand sparks were swept across the window. Instinctively we knew that in one of the west wings a roof had fallen in.

Hark! What was that? A voice was calling—a girl's shrill voice, it sounded almost like a child's. Whence did the cry come? It was nowhere in the house. Yet it could hardly be outside.

"Help! Quick! *Quick! My God! Help!*" The door of the room creaked ominously. Phew! The heat in the passage was scorching it. In a minute it would burst into flame. Where was that voice? I rushed to the window—

"*Hello! Hello!*" I shouted at the top of my voice.

The cry came from above. Tightly clutching the window frame I leapt forward and peered up in the darkness. As I did so, a coil of stout rope fell past me and disappeared. Now a rope was hanging down across the window from above. I stretched out an arm, and was just able to clutch it.

"Is it fast?" I shouted.

"Yes—fast to an iron staple that supports the chimney. Get out, quick! Quick!"

"Go down first—go down!" I shouted up.

"*I tell you to get out!*" the girl's voice cried. This was no time for courtesies. The girl said we must go, and so...

I was pulled back violently from the window and flung on to the floor. A man was clutching at the rope. It was Paulton. At the same instant a shout of laughter sounded in the room. Scrambling to my feet, I saw Faulkner laughing. Had the man any nerves at all? Did he know what fear meant?

"Paulton did that," he exclaimed. "I think he's the limit. Look at him sliding down—the cur! Who is the girl above?"

"I don't know, and don't care!" I cried. "Do for the love of Heaven, follow down. I'm suffocating. The fire will be on us in an instant."

"And leave the girl!" he said in a tone of reproach and surprise. "You can't mean it, Ashton."

"She won't go first—she said so."

"Won't she?"

He went over to the window, leaned out as I had done, and looked up as best he could.

"Go down at once," he shouted in a tone of extraordinary firmness. "We don't move until you do."

I suppose his commanding tone made her realise he really meant to wait. Anyway, a moment later a girl's figure appeared, swinging above the window. She rested her feet upon the window-sill, and looked at us.

"Don't be frightened," she said. "It is tied very firmly, and the staple can't give way."

"Don't be frightened!" And this from the "chit of a girl," as I had called her the night before when she had so cleverly induced us to stay in the room. She was just visible now in the blackness beneath, as she slid down the rope with remarkable agility.

"Go ahead, Ashton," Faulkner said, as the rope slackened. "I'll steady the rope while you go down. Don't get excited! There's lots of time."

Smoke was floating up from the window now as though the window were a chimney. My smarting eyes met Faulkner's as I clutched the rope with both hands and prepared to swing out. His eyes were bloodshot, red and swollen. Yet he was actually smiling. And he had lit another cigarette!

It was with a feeling of intense relief, that as I looked up from the ground, I saw Faulkner swing out on the rope from the fourth storey window, twisting round and round like a joint upon a roasting jack. It is said that in moments of acute crisis thoughts, absurd in their triviality, sometimes take prominence. It was so now. As I watched, with halting breath, Faulkner's hunched-up figure slowly sliding down like a monkey on a string, only one thought was in my mind.

Would he, when he reached the ground, have that cigarette between his lips?

He reached the ground, and I went up to him. In an access of emotion I grasped him by the hand.

"You are a hero, old chap!" I exclaimed. "A perfect hero!"

"Don't be foolish, Ashton," he answered. "Instead, hand out that box of matches. I do think," he added, "it might have occurred to you to hang on to the rope to prevent my spinning round in that absurd fashion. I hate being made to look ridiculous."

He struck a match. Yes, the cigarette was still between his lips!

I had never before seen a blazing house at close quarters, and the sight impressed though it appalled me. Together we walked out into the weedy Italian garden, a hundred yards or more, and there stood watching the spectacle. Truly, it was superb. One after another immense sheets of flame shot up high into the sky, parted into fifty tongues which quivered for an instant, then vanished.

Where was Vera? What of her? Was she still alive, or had she died in that awful furnace?

A breeze was at our backs, and thus the smoke was swept away, revealing the conflagration in all its awful grandeur.

And now the window we had just left began suddenly to turn red. The redness grew brighter. As I watched it, panting with excitement, a red and yellow ribbon licked the window frame that a few minutes previously we had clutched. The ribbon broadened, lengthened, swept out into the night, lapping the grey wall of the old château until it floated high above the roof, shrivelling the ivy and burning it to ashes.

That was the last window in the main building. There was nothing more to burn. For some moments the flames seemed slightly to subside. Then, all at once, with a great crash which must surely have been heard a mile or more away, the entire roof broke inward, opening up to the sky an inferno from which blazing fragments in their thousands and myriad sparks shooting up into the sky illuminated fields and woods for several miles around.

"What a gorgeous sight!"

It was the middle of the night, and the place being far removed from any habitation save the little village two miles off behind the hill, the alarm had not yet been raised.

I turned. Faulkner's eyes, wide open, were rivetted on the scene. For the first time in his life, as I believe, he had given way to his emotion. "Ah!" he added in an undertone, "how this makes one think!"

"Think?" I said. "Of what?" My only thought was of my loved one.

He turned his head and looked at me.

"Oh," he answered cynically, "of what we shall have for lunch to-morrow. Good Heavens!" he exclaimed, and in the light cast down upon us by the blood-red canopy flickering in the sky above I could see his eyes shining strangely, "Have you no sense at all of grandeur? Can't you realise and appreciate the overpowering magnificence of all this? Have you no sentiment, romance or poetry at all in your conception? Don't you feel the hand of Providence? Doesn't this bring home to you the majesty of eternity better than any religion that has been tried or thought of? Really, Ashton, really..."

I was amazed at his sudden outburst of pent-up feeling—I had imagined him cold, undemonstrative, unemotional, a being without nerves and devoid of temperament. So his self-control and apparent calmness had been nothing but a mask. I think I liked him all the better for it.

We heard voices—women's shrill, terrified voices. We were unable to locate them. Suddenly I started. Surely that was Vera's voice! Yes, I recognised it.

Attentively we both listened. Then, as the flames shot up again, lighting up the meadows away to the woods, we both distinctly saw in silhouette a man and a woman struggling in the distance.

The man had her by the wrists. He was overpowering her. At that same moment the red glare sank, and both were hidden in the darkness.

Chapter Seventeen.

Found in the Débris.

We were on the alert in a moment.

Though we searched in the darkness for a distance of a hundred yards or more, we failed to come upon either the man or the woman of whom we had caught a brief glimpse as they struggled desperately.

Nor did we again hear the sound of voices. That I had heard Vera's voice, I felt convinced. We wondered if there was a lodge, and how far it was away. Perhaps the servants had taken shelter there.

"The whole place seems to be deserted," Faulkner said when, after a futile search, we again found ourselves near the burning château, where the fire had by this time subsided considerably. "And yet there must have been people in the house—at any rate, servants."

We walked right round the château. What a huge old place it had been! No wonder the fire had taken a long time to reach us, if it had broken out, as it presumably had done, in a wing remote from the room where we had been. Judging by the architecture of the outer walls I concluded that the château must have been built towards the end of the fourteenth century, and afterwards added to.

There was a sharp nip in the air, and we felt chilly enough. Already the streaks of dawn were striving to pierce the belt of leaden clouds, against which the black pinewoods could be seen distinctly outlined.

Faulkner turned to me.

"Have you any money?" he asked.

"Plenty," I answered. "Why?"

"When it is daylight we must make for the nearest village and get a conveyance to the railway-station. We must be miles from everywhere, or fire-escapes would have come along before now. I suppose the Baronne is dead."

"She can have escaped only by a miracle," I said. "We shall probably know soon."

"And that cur—Paulton. What can have become of him?"

"I can't help thinking it was Paulton we saw struggling. But who can the woman have been? I hope it wasn't Vera. I am certain I heard her voice. What do you think?"

"It may have been Mademoiselle de Coudron," Faulkner said. "She seems to have disappeared. What a brave girl! She must have climbed along the roofs to save us, with the fire just behind her. I wonder who the woman was who called for help first of all—I mean before we knew that fire had broken out."

"The whole thing is most mysterious, but the biggest mystery is the disappearance of everybody. We heard at least three voices in the darkness!"

Happening to glance down the long carriage drive which, after winding for a hundred yards across the broad, level lawns, disappeared into the wood, I noticed two men on horseback approaching at a walk. They had just emerged from the wood, and, so far as I could see in the half-light, were officials of some kind.

They broke into a jog-trot as they caught sight of us, and took a short cut across the grass. As they came near us we saw that they were two gendarmes.

"What are you doing here?" one of them asked sharply in French.

I didn't like his tone, and I saw Faulkner's lip twitch with annoyance. Instead of answering, we looked the two men up and down.

"What are you doing here—tell me at once," the speaker repeated, in a bullying tone.

I suppose we did look disreputable, standing there without collars, with unlaced boots, and with our coat collars turned up. Also a day's growth of beard is hardly conducive to a smart appearance, and in most civilised countries but America a man is judged by his appearance and by the clothes he wears.

"Who set fire to the château?" demanded the gendarme, quickly losing his temper as we refused to speak.

"Oh, we did, of course," I exclaimed in French, meaning to be cynical. "We burnt it down on purpose."

The man raised his black eyebrows, and glanced at his companion.

"You hear that?" he said meaningly.

The man who had remained silent produced a notebook and scribbled in it.

Faulkner turned to me.

"A few more of your 'witticisms' Ashton," he said, "and we shall get penal servitude. Don't you know you are talking to State officials, and have you ever known a State official to be other than matter-of-fact? For Heaven's sake, don't make more statements that may be used in evidence against us."

"My friend was joking," Faulkner said in his perfect French to the man who had addressed us; but the official seemed not to understand what the word *plaisanterie* meant.

At this juncture the men exchanged one or two remarks in a rapid undertone. Then, while one of them remained, apparently to keep guard over us, the other cantered away across the turf, struck the road close to the wood, and disappeared.

In the absence of his companion, who apparently was his superior in authority, the gendarme thawed to some extent. We gathered that the Château d'Uzerche was about eighty miles by road from Monte Carlo, and twelve or so miles from Digne, in the Bedeone Valley, also that no village lay within a radius of two miles of it. Small wonder, therefore, that no fire-escape had come.

"Where is la Baronne de Coudron?" the man asked suddenly.

We explained that we feared she had been either burnt or suffocated. At this he looked grave.

"And her companion, the Englishman Monsieur Paulton, where is he?"

Again we explained. He had escaped from the fire, but, since his escape, we had not seen him.

"Why do you want to know?" Faulkner asked, in his politest tones.

"Because," the man answered, taken off his guard, "we have a warrant for the arrest of both Madame la Baronne and the Englishman."

"Arrest! For what?" Faulkner asked.

"On several charges. The most recent is a charge of obtaining money by fraud—a large sum. There is also a charge of blackmail."

"Against both?"

"Against both."

I was silent. Here was a new phase of the affair. By degrees we gathered from him that Paulton was known to be interested in various undertakings of, to say the least, a dubious nature, also that he promoted wild-cat companies in England, on the Continent, and in America. Information that especially interested us was that all who had escaped from the fire had made their way to the lodge at the entrance to the drive.

It was at this juncture that the other gendarme reappeared. He was still on horseback, and, as he came towards us slowly, our attention became centred upon the man who walked beside him, with one hand on his stirrup. In the distance it looked very like Paulton.

He seemed quite composed. His mouth was bound up, partly concealing his face.

When a few yards from us the gendarme reined up. As he did so, Paulton raised his arm, pointed at me, and said in French—

"That's the man you came to arrest. That is Dago Paulton."

"And his companion?" the gendarme asked.

"Is his valet."

"And your name, monsieur?"

"Ferrari—Paoli Ferrari. My father was Italian, my mother English. I have been in Mr Paulton's service as butler for the last three years. Previous to that I was butler to Count Pinto"—the Portuguese diplomat who had won the cup for shooting.

"Thank you, monsieur, I am exceedingly indebted to you," the gendarme said blandly. Then, producing an official-looking document, he said to me—

"We have to take you into custody, you and Madame la Baronne."

For some moments, indignation prevented my speaking. Was it possible these outrageous statements of Paulton's would be taken without question? Such a thing seemed monstrous and grotesque, but knowing, as I did, how intensely stupid some police officials are, no matter to what country they may belong, I thought it likely that I should presently be marched off and placed under lock and key.

Faulkner, to my annoyance, seemed amused.

"They will march you twelve miles to Digne," he said, "and when you get there and prove your identity they will apologise in the most humble fashion for the mistake that has been made. Meanwhile, you will have had your twelve-mile walk, and Paulton have been allowed to escape. Had we looked less disreputable than we do, our statements might have been believed in preference to his."

In my indignation I at first became sarcastic, and thinking that liberty at that moment would be far better than being held up upon a false charge, I made a sudden bolt for it, cutting swiftly across a meadow and leaping a stream. I am a good runner, but, of course, the mounted gendarmes were quickly upon me, and cut me off, so I soon found myself in their hands.

Faulkner elected to come with me, but we were not marched to Digne. Instead, we were allowed to walk leisurely alongside the horses as far as the village, a distance of two miles or so, and there were shown into a comfortable room in the tiny police bureau, and given breakfast. The garde-champêtre spoke English fluently. He had lived in England several years. Consequently in a short time we succeeded in convincing him of the blunder the gendarme had made, and in proving who we were.

By this time the village was beginning to awaken, and crowds were on their way to the château. We soon found a tradesman willing to let out a horse and trap in return for a louis paid in advance. In this we also started back for the château, anxious to get news of Vera, and of Violet.

On our way by the road, we found the lodge of the château, it had not been in sight more than a minute, when a large red car passed out through the gateway into the high road we were on, turned, and sped away from us along the long white ribbon of road at terrific speed. It must, we calculated as it dwindled into a distant speck, have been travelling at a speed of quite sixty miles an hour. Faulkner looked at me significantly. Our surmise had been correct, the servants had sought shelter at the lodge and had now left.

By the time we reached the smouldering ruins, a score of people, all of them peasants, stood staring at it. The good French farmers had each some platitude to make: "It must have been an enormous fire;" "It must have burned very quickly;" "Some one must have set it alight," and so on. They were all people of the bovine type, as we found when we tried to obtain information from them.

The Baronne and her niece lived there. That was about all that they could tell us. Apparently they knew nothing of Paulton—had never seen or heard of him.

How many servants had there been in the Château they knew not. But a man and several women had just left the lodge in a motor-car.

"We can do no good by staying here," Faulkner said at last. "We had better make for Digne. What puzzles me is, where can the servants be? There must have been servants, and they could have told us something. They are not at the lodge. Perhaps Paulton had taken them with him in the car we had seen. The only soul at the lodge is an old woman who is stone deaf, and she is crying so that she cannot speak at all."

We stood gazing thoughtfully at the still smouldering fire, when Faulkner said suddenly—

"What is that big, square thing down among the twisted girders?" and he pointed to it.

We could not make out what it was. Then, all at once I realised.

"Why," I said, "it's a safe—one of those big American safes. I expect its contents are uninjured."

But where was Vera? Ah! I felt beside myself in anxiety—a breathless, burning longing, to know how fared the one woman in all the world who held me in her hands for life, or for death.

She loved me, truly and well—of that I was convinced. And yet she existed in that mysterious hateful bondage—a bondage which, alas! she dared not attempt to break.

What could be the truth? Why were her lips closed?—Ay, why indeed? I dreaded to think.

Chapter Eighteen.

In which the Mask is Raised.

Three days had passed.

Two curious things happened while we were sitting in the atrium of the Casino in Monte Carlo during the interval.

In the first place Paulton's friend, Henderson, whom I had met only on that one occasion in the fumoir of the hotel, happened to saunter in. He looked hard at both of us, but either did not recognise us—a thing that I think hardly possible—or else deliberately cut us.

Later, I went over to the buffet with Faulkner, for the play was not interesting, and we had decided to leave. A dozen men stood there, talking, and suddenly I caught the word "D'Uzerche."

They were talking of the fire three days previously. Anxious to hear all I could about Château d'Uzerche, I moved a little nearer.

"They've not discovered the Baronne's body," I heard the young Frenchman say, "and apparently no one else was burnt. I wonder if those old rumours one heard about the Baronne were really true?"

"What rumours?" his companion, a bald-headed gambler, asked. "I don't seem to remember hearing any."

"You mean to say you have never heard the stories that everybody knows?" the first speaker exclaimed. "My dear fellow, where do you live?"

"In Paris as a rule," his friend answered drily. "I returned here last week."

"Ah, pardon me, I had forgotten. Well, it has long been common talk—"

He lowered his voice and spoke into his companion's ear. I approached as near as I dared, but I could not catch a word.

"You can't mean it!" his friend exclaimed. "Surely it isn't possible!"

"Everything is possible, *mon cher ami*," the first speaker said. "The less possible things seem, generally the more possible they are. I shall be anxious to hear what is found inside the safe that the newspapers say has been discovered amongst the débris. If it is not claimed it will, I take it, be the duty of the police to open it."

"But surely it will be claimed."

"I doubt it under the circumstances. I believe the rumours to be true."

An electric bell rang arrogantly, in warning that the curtain was about to rise, and some moments later the atrium was half deserted.

I told Faulkner what I had heard. He seemed in no way surprised.

"I thought it inadvisable to tell you this before," he said after a pause, "but now that you have got wind of it I may as well tell you the rumours—or rather the chief one. The rest don't matter. The Baronne de Coudron was known to be extremely rich, yet a few years ago she was quite poor. She bought the Château d'Uzerche recently. How and where she suddenly got the money is a mystery that has puzzled everybody, and rumours have been afloat that she obtained it by means which could lead her to penal servitude. But of course nobody knows anything definite—so nobody dares do more than insinuate."

"The gendarmes seemed to know something definite," I said.

"Yes, and much use they made of it! Paulton is most likely safely back in England by now."

"They can arrest him there of course."

"They can—but will they? Do you think officials capable of being hoodwinked as these gendarmes were, will have acumen enough to catch a clever man like Paulton? We must admit that he is clever."

The more I saw of Faulkner, the more I grew to like him. Singularly undemonstrative in ordinary conversation, he recalled to my mind a blacksmith's forge that is covered and banked up with cold, wet coal, but that burns so fiercely within. What had first attracted me to the lad had been his amazing coolness in the face of death, a coolness that amounted to indifference. I could picture him under fire, calmly rolling a cigarette and telling others what to do. Yet he was not a soldier. Like myself he was merely an idler. Leaving out the Houghton Park incident, I have myself only once been under fire. It was not on a battlefield, though not far from one—the field of Tewkesbury. It was during a big rabbit shoot, when two of the guns fired straight at me simultaneously, and the rabbit they killed rolled over on to my feet, dead.

My conduct was not heroic on that occasion I am afraid. With one bound I sprang behind a big elm, and, from that position of safety, hurled vituperation at my unintentional assailants, ordering them to desist. It took me some moments to convince myself I had not been hit, but the shock to my system was, I confess, considerable.

From the theatre we strolled through the big doors into the Salles de jeux. I tossed a hundred-franc note on the rouge and left it there. Red came up six times, and I gathered up my winnings.

The ball clicked again the seventh time, and black came up!

An old man with fingers like claws, and horribly long and dirty nails, introduced himself, engaged me in conversation, and ended by trying to induce me to partake in his infallible system for winning at roulette!

What a lot of rubbish has been written about the Rooms at Monte! The first time I went there—when I was quite a youth—I expected to find a sort of Aladdin's palace, myriad glittering lights everywhere, gorgeously-dressed women sparkling with diadems and precious stones.

Instead, I sauntered into a series of large, lofty, heavily-gilded rooms with an atmosphere one could cut with a knife, in which were several long tables with people sitting round them, quite common-looking people, and anything but smart; the majority of the women were bloused and skirted tourists. One might have mistaken the scene for a number of board-meetings in progress simultaneously, but for the fact that in the centre of each table sat men in funereal black who, at intervals, droned monotonously through their noses—

"*Messieurs, faites vos jeux.*"

And then a little later—

"*Rien n'va plus!*"

Then the click of the ball, and the jingle of money lost and won.

It was one of the greatest disillusionments I have ever experienced. There was nothing in the least exciting, nothing sensational. There was a rustle of notes, and the whole scene was sordid, debasing. I can remember only one other disillusionment that has given me so great a shock. I experienced that the first time I visited Niagara Falls. I had seen pictures in plenty of the Falls, and had based thereon my idea of what the Falls would look like when I got there.

I arrived at noon, eager to gaze upon "Nature's Marvellous Phenomenon," as the booklet of the Railway Company described it. The first thing I saw was a truly gigantic hoarding-board advertising somebody's lung-tonic, alongside it one recommending some one else's Blood Capsules, and then, whichever way I looked, the landscape, which should have been gorgeous, was disfigured by similar announcements. Even the water was spoilt, for some of the falls being harnessed to dye-works, ran in shades of dirty greens and reds and yellows, and when I wanted to go under the main Falls I found I must buy a ticket at a box-office and go down in a lift. Never, I remember thinking, have the words, "Where only man is vile," been more applicable than at Niagara.

But this is an aside. Elated at my success at roulette, a game which generally bores me, for I generally lose, I suggested to Faulkner that we should go together to some haunt of amusement more exhilarating than the Casino.

"What about the ball down in La Condamine to-night?" he asked, looking at me oddly.

"Ball?" I said. "What ball? I didn't know there was one."

"Oh, yes there is. It isn't an aristocratic ball, you know. Far from it. I've lived out here a good deal, and got to know my way about. It is rather an expensive form of amusement, but as you have made two hundred and fifty-six pounds in ten minutes, you may as well spend a pound or two that way as any other. I think you will afterwards admit it has been an 'experience'."

I did admit it—and a great deal besides. It was the most "unconventional" ball I had ever attended, or have attended since. We picked up a number of acquaintances, eight or ten in all, and went boisterously down to La Condamine. The gay supper was most enjoyable. Most of the women's dresses were suitable for warm climates, being conspicuous by their scantiness, rather than by their beauty. Some wore the black *loup* over their eyes. At supper I sat beside a girl whose identity was thus concealed. She had a wonderful figure, and her thick dark hair hung in two long plaits down below her waist. About her movements there was something that seemed familiar to me, and in vain I tried to recollect when I had met her before, and where. At last my curiosity outran my discretion.

"Take off your mask," I said to her in French. "I'll give you two louis."

"Give them to me," she said, also in French, the only language she had talked, "and I will take it off."

I did so.

"Don't be too surprised," she exclaimed in broken English with a ripple of laughter. She pulled up the mask, then twisted it off, and I found myself seated beside Lady Thorold's maid, Judith, whom I had last seen at the hotel on the night the Baronne de Coudron had arrived.

I confess that I was considerably annoyed.

I am not, I am thankful to think, one of those men who like to behave absurdly with domestic servants, especially with other people's servants.

I had never liked this girl, she had always struck me as being hypocritical and designing, and though now she looked extremely pretty, judged by a certain standard, I could not dispel from my thoughts the picture of the demure maid with downcast eyes, whom a casual observer probably would not have looked at twice.

Her manner was the reverse of demure, nor were her eyes downcast. They struck me as being the most brazen eyes I had seen for a long time as they gazed unflinchingly up into my own. Much as I knew, I disliked her, I could not, at that moment, help noticing those strangely dark eyes of hers, now so full of laughter and wickedness; also the singular evenness of the small white teeth; the natural redness of the full lips; the clear, olive complexion, and the thick mantle of long, blue-black hair. Yet I did not admire her in the least. Oh, no. If her appearance struck me as remarkable and not wholly unpleasing, it was only for a brief instant.

"Have you left Lady Thorold's service?" I asked, loud enough for others to hear. I thought that, at any rate, would be a nasty snub. Instead, she laughed immoderately. So, to my surprise, did her friends who had overheard my question.

"Ah, monsieur, but you are too *drôle*!" she exclaimed, as she stopped laughing. "I was not in Lady Thorold's service, or in la Baronne de Coudron's or in anybody else's. I have never been in service. I—in service? I? Pah!"

She made a gesture of contempt.

"I don't understand," I said.

"I was Lady Thorold's friend, her very intimate friend, and la Baronne de Coudron's too, and—and other people's. I am no *servant*, I assure you! m'sieur."

I stared at her.

"You little impostor!" I said after a pause.

She laughed, and took my arm confidingly.

"I have always liked you, I have really," she said in a coaxing undertone. "You are not like other men. You are not always trying to make love to everybody. *Ma foi*! How I detest some of your countrymen, they make themselves too ridiculous when they come to France."

"You seem to know a lot about them," I answered, for want of something better to say.

"*Bien*! I can assure you!" she replied, to my surprise, quite bitterly. Then she said quickly, in her broken English as though anxious to change the subject—

"You want Mademoiselle Vera—eh?"

"What do you mean?" I gasped, amazed.

"What I say. You want her. Well, she is quite near here."

"Near here!"

"*Mais oui.* Pay me enough, and I will take you to her—now."

I was panting with excitement. With an effort I controlled myself. It was clear to me that this woman knew a great deal. She might indeed be able to clear up the whole mystery of Houghton Park if she were paid enough, perhaps also the mystery connected with Château d'Uzerche.

Yes, I would humour her. If it became necessary, I would pay her the highest sum she might ask for, that I was in a position to pay. But first to meet my darling again. How I longed to see her once more, after all those mysterious happenings!

"How much do you want?" I asked abruptly.

She named an absurdly large sum. Eventually we came to terms, and I paid her in French notes.

"*Très bien!*" she said, as she stuffed the money into some queer corner in her brief skirt. "You are a gentilhomme, not like ze others. *Mais oui.*"

Then she rose, signalled to me with her eyes, and I followed her out of the room.

Chapter Nineteen.

More Revelations.

Eagerly I strode out after her.

We went a short distance along the road to the left, then turned again to the left and halted before a large white house. Up two flights of stairs she led me, along a short corridor, and through two rooms. She opened the door at the further end of the second room, and then motioned to me to enter.

Seated at a table, playing cards, were Paulton, Violet de Coudron, Vera Thorold and the Baronne. Violet and Vera were in evening gowns—Vera in turquoise blue. The sight of the Baronne sitting there, alive and uninjured, so astounded me that I remained speechless. Paulton sprang fiercely to his feet.

"Who brought you up here?" he exclaimed furiously. "Who?"

The door had remained open. A ripple of laughter behind me made me cast a hurried glance that way, and I saw Judith convulsed with amusement. She recovered her composure in a few moments, and came in.

"I have carried out my threat," she said in French quickly, addressing Paulton. "You brought it entirely upon yourself by your niggardliness. Mr Ashton is generous—and a gentilhomme."

Paulton clenched his fist.

"Yes," the French girl went on, looking at him fearlessly, "you are quite right to restrain yourself. It would be a bad night's work if a tragedy were to happen *here*. At the château it was different. You had it your own way there—up to a point."

The man became blasphemous, and I saw Vera wince. Her eyes were set upon mine, in mute appeal.

The truth flashed in upon me. Paulton ran this private gaming establishment. The Baronne presumably was his partner. Judith was an accomplice. But the two girls? What part did they play? It was horrible finding Vera here, yet my faith in her never wavered. I knew she must be there against her will, that eventually she would explain all. And seeing what I had seen of Violet, I felt equally sure that circumstances which she too could not prevent were responsible for her presence.

I suppose most men who self-complacently term themselves "men of the world," would have laughed outright at what they would have called my "blind belief in innocence," had the circumstances been related to them. For here were two young girls mixing with the lost souls of Monte Carlo, and apparently enjoying themselves. On the face of it, my confidence seemed quixotic, I admit, but there are times when I trust my instinct rather than even circumstantial evidence. And up to now my instinct has generally proved correct.

This was no time for deliberate thought, however. I knew I must act quickly, and for once I was able to come to a decision with remarkable promptitude. Obviously Paulton and the Baronne were there in hiding. They knew they were liable at any moment to be arrested. And, thanks to Judith, I had discovered their place of concealment.

"You know there is a warrant out for the arrest of you both," I said, facing them fearlessly. "I can at once inform the police of your whereabouts—or I can say nothing. It is for you to decide which I shall do."

The Baronne looked at me, as I thought, imploringly.

"If Vera Thorold comes away with me at once, and you undertake never again to molest her, your secret will remain safe, so far as I am concerned. If you refuse to let her come, then you will be arrested at once."

The tables were, indeed, strangely turned. A few days previously these two adventurers had held me at their mercy, and Faulkner too. Now I could dictate to them what terms I chose.

I saw a look of dismay enter Violet de Coudron's eyes, and I guessed the reason of it. She and Vera had become close friends, and now Vera was to go from her. It seemed dreadful to leave a young, beautiful, refined girl like Violet in the control of these ghouls, yet I could not suggest their surrendering her too, for was she not the Baronne's niece? And was the Baronne actually a Baronne—or was she merely an adventuress? I had looked up her name and family in the "Almanack de Gotha," and she seemed to be all right, but still—

Then an idea came to me. I would, with Vera's help, and Faulkner's, try to steal the girl away if she should express a wish to leave those unhealthy and unholy surroundings. It would be almost like repaying Paulton and the Baronne in their own coin. These and other thoughts sped through my mind with great rapidity.

"Well," I said quickly, addressing Paulton again, "what is your answer? Am I to betray your whereabouts, or not?"

He still hesitated, still loth to decide. Then suddenly he exclaimed abruptly—

"Take her. I shall be even with you soon, never fear. I shall be even with you in a way you don't expect."

I smiled, thinking his words were but a hollow taunt. Later, however, I also realised to the full that his had been no empty boast.

The two girls left the room, and both returned wearing hats and sealskin coats over their evening gowns. Then, linking my arm in that of my beloved, we descended the stairs together.

At last she was saved from that scoundrelly gang who seemed to hold her so completely in their clutches, she was still mine—mine!

At Judith's suggestion we walked back to where the ball was in progress. As a matter-of-fact I was undecided how next to act. Besides, I wanted to see Faulkner, who was awaiting me.

So we went back, and seated with Vera and Judith, I had a long chat with the latter, about many things. She told me much that interested me. Paulton and the Baronne ran this establishment, as I had guessed, and often made it their headquarters. They had several assumed names. They had run similar secret gaming-houses in Paris, Ostend, Aix and elsewhere. In this particular house they lived in a big, well-furnished flat overlooking the harbour of Monaco. Vera and Violet had each a bedroom, and shared a sitting-room. Since they had met for the first time, some weeks previously, they had become great friends—in fact almost inseparable. Both had been staying at the Château d'Uzerche when the fire had broken out, and she, Judith, had been there too. It had been Vera's voice we had heard calling for help before we suspected the alarming truth. She had been overcome by smoke in her own room—it was just before that she had called for help—and almost stifled. No lives had been lost. There had been only five servants at D'Uzerche that night, and they had all escaped. The Baronne had, it seemed, escaped by turning sharp to the right into a lumber-room, almost directly she had rushed out of the room. From the lumber-room she had scrambled through a skylight on to the roof, entered another skylight immediately above a rusty iron fire staircase, the existence of which everybody else had forgotten, and so made her way out of the building in safety.

I inquired about the man and woman struggling in the dark.

She smiled when I referred to this, and, pulling up her short sleeve—it reached barely to her elbow—displayed several horizontal streaks of a deep purple which looked like bruises.

"I was that woman," exclaimed Judith quietly. "The man was Dago, and these are the marks his fingers left upon me when he gripped me and fought with me. Are you surprised I have to-night so readily betrayed his hiding-place?"

"Not so very readily," I said, thinking of the sum of which she had mulcted me before she would speak at all.

Guessing my thoughts, she laughed.

"Still, m'sieur," she said, "you will admit that you have received full value for your money, *n'est-ce-pas?*"

During this conversation, carried on in one of the ante-rooms within earshot of the music in the ballroom, Vera sat almost in silence. I grew to understand the woman Judith better, indeed almost to like her. She said little about herself, though I questioned her frequently concerning her own life. She seemed more inclined to talk of other people, and their doings. One thing I did gather was that she belonged to a gang of male and female adventurers, who probably stood at nothing when they had an end to gain. To this gang belonged also the Baronne, Paulton and Henderson. Whether Sir Charles Thorold was, or was not, in some way mixed up in this gang's schemes I could not ascertain for certain, though several times I tried to. For about Sir Charles and Lady Thorold, Judith seemed unwilling to speak.

I had a long and confidential chat with Vera. Ah! that hour was perhaps full of the sweetest happiness of my life. She was mine—mine! It was past three in the morning when we paused for a few moments in our animated conversation. "Ah, here comes your friend," exclaimed my sweet beloved.

Faulkner, passing the open door, had caught sight of us and strolled in. Violet de Coudron was with him. She looked dreadfully tired, I thought, though this did not greatly detract from her very exceptional beauty.

Briefly, I told Faulkner all that had happened.

"It is fortunate we are not conventional," he said lightly, when I had outlined my plan. "What food for scandal some people would find in all this. I think, after all, that our visit here to-night has not been wholly unprofitable—eh? You may be surprised to hear that this new friend of mine"—and he indicated Violet de Coudron, seated beside him—"has arranged to leave the Baronne for good and all. She tells me she leads an awful life here, and that when Vera is gone—"

"But you have known Vera only a few weeks," I interrupted, addressing Violet.

"Yes," she answered sadly, with her pretty accent, "and those are the only weeks of comparative happiness I have had. I couldn't stay here with these people without her. I couldn't. I really couldn't. Oh, if you only knew all I have been through—all I have been forced to endure since the Baronne adopted me!" And she hid her face in her hands.

"Adopted you!" I exclaimed. "You said you were the Baronne's niece."

"I said so—yes. I always said so, because she made me, and I passed always as her niece. But I am not. I can scarcely remember my parents. All I can recollect is that they were very poor—but oh, so kind to me! I remember their kissing me passionately one day, with tears streaming down their cheeks—it was evening, and nearly dark—and telling me that they had to go away from me, that probably we should never meet again in this world."

"How old were you then?" I asked, much interested.

"I could not have been more than six, possibly seven. It was in Rouen. They took me to a big, fashionable street I did not remember having ever been in before, kissed me again and again once more, stood me by the *porte-cochère*, and rang the bell. Then they went hurriedly away. By the time the bell was answered, they had disappeared. I was questioned by a tall man-servant—after that, I don't exactly recollect what happened, except that the Baronne adopted me. She lived in the big house."

"And it was in Rouen, you say?"

"Yes, in Rouen."

"Do you think you would recognise it if you saw the outside of it again?" I asked quickly.

She paused.

"I think I should," she said thoughtfully, "though we did not stay there long—not more than a few months. Why do you ask?"

"Only," I answered, "because I have an idea. But now let us leave this place. It is nearly four o'clock."

Yes, we were a truly unconventional quartette.

The hotel people were surprised, on the following morning, to find one of our two rooms occupied by two fair visitors, while in the other Faulkner and I slept, tucked up together. But in gay, reckless Monte nobody is surprised at anything.

That an attempt would at once be made to discover Violet's whereabouts and get her back, we knew. For that reason we had arranged to leave for Paris by the mid-day *rapide*.

Chapter Twenty.

Concerns a Mysterious Light.

London—the dear, dirty old city of delight—looked gloomy enough as we passed out of Charing Cross yard, and made our way around the corner to the *Grand Hotel*. It was a damp, raw evening, and after the crisp atmosphere and bright sunshine of the Riviera, seemed to us more than ordinarily depressing.

By wire we had engaged rooms at the *Grand* for Vera and Violet, overlooking Trafalgar Square, and we now began to wonder what our next step ought to be. I wanted, if possible, to get into communication with Sir Charles and Lady Thorold, for I was anxious not to delay my marriage any longer, and Vera, though she had promised to become my wife as soon as possible, refused to do so until she had seen her parents.

But where were her parents?

She had no idea, neither had I. We had telegraphed to the address in Brighton where they had been staying, but an intimation had come from the Post Office that the message had not been delivered, the addressee having left.

As for Faulkner, he was distrait. Something seemed to be on his mind, and I thought I knew what it was. He was engaged to be married to Gladys Deroxe, of whom Vera had, during the past day or two, let drop certain things.

Gladys Deroxe, she had confided to me among other things, was one of the most jealous women she had ever met. Her jealousy amounted almost to an obsession. When I heard this I breathed a fervent hope that Faulkner might never marry her, for I have seen something of jealous wives among my friends. What was weighing upon Faulkner's mind, of course, was that he had brought Violet to London with him, and that, as Miss Deroxe lived in Mayfair, she might at any moment get to hear of this, and then?

Another thought occurred to me now, for the first time. Had my unemotional, phlegmatic friend fallen in love with Violet de Coudron, the foundling?

She was pretty and fascinating enough for any one to fall in love with. Personally, I thought Faulkner would do well to marry her in preference to Gladys, who I gathered to be something of a schemer, with an eye to the main chance. Vera had come to know Miss Deroxe quite by accident. At first she had liked her, but soon she had begun to discover her true character. Violet on the contrary, she liked immensely. Yet girls form strange prejudices.

Thus a week of anxiety passed. The two girls remained at the *Grand*, while I stayed at my rooms, and Faulkner slept at his club. Though he did not tell me, I knew he had not informed Gladys of his return to town. Therefore he must have felt somewhat perturbed, though, as was his wont, he completely hid his feelings, when one morning as I was walking with him up Hamilton Place a taxi swept up behind us, stopped beside the kerb, and a rather florid-looking girl, leaning out of the cab window, called in a loud, querulous voice—

"Frank! *Frank!*"

Before he presented me to her I had guessed her identity, and I saw at a glance that she was none too well pleased at his being in London without her knowing it.

"I was calling upon my uncle Henry," she said presently, "and chanced to look out of the window, when I saw you go by. I was amazed. I thought you were on the Riviera still. So I hurried out, hailed a taxi, and pursued you. Why didn't you tell me you were back?"

He invented on the spot some excellent reason—I forget what it was—and it seemed to satisfy her. And then, feeling that my presence was not needed, I made an excuse, raised my hat, and left them.

"I am only glad," I remembered saying mentally and ungrammatically, "it is Faulkner, and not I, who is to marry that girl."

Next day, I took my well-beloved in the car down to Virginia Water, where we lunched, and returned in the afternoon. That evening I, as usual, scanned the personal columns of the *Morning Post*. I have a habit of doing this, as some of the announcements one sees there are not devoid of humour.

That day the personal columns were singularly dull. The advertisements of money-lenders masquerading as private gentlemen, and as ladies anxious to be philanthropic, occupied a good deal of the space. There was the widow of twenty-three who implored "some kind-hearted gentleman" (sic) "to lend her twenty pounds to save her from the bailiffs;" a "lady of high social standing, closely related to an Earl," who touted for the chaperonage of débutantes, willing to pay for the privilege of being surreptitiously smuggled into Society; a crack-brained inventor advertising for some one to finance a new torpedo for destroying German bands, or something of the kind, and so on. There was nothing at all exciting. Why, I can't say, but quite a commonplace line at the foot of the second column interested me. It ran—

"*Meet me 2.*"

That was all—no name, no address, no date. Why I had noticed it at all, I could not imagine. I concluded it must be the extreme brevity of the advertisement that had caught my fancy.

Next morning, it being dry and fine, I called at the *Grand Hotel*, and took Vera for a run in the car to Hatfield, returning by St. Albans. We lunched at Pagani's—one gets so tired of the sameness of the ordinary restaurants—and after that I left Vera at the hotel, and sent my car to the garage.

Somehow I felt in a restless mood, and the atmosphere of well-bred respectability pervading the club oppressed me, as it so often does. I am afraid that the older I grow the more Bohemian I become, and the less willing to bend to convention. It seems to me farcical, for instance, that in this twentieth century of ours, a rule made fifty years ago to the effect that "pipes shall not be smoked in this club," should still be enforced. Plenty of the younger members of the clubs where this rule obtains have endeavoured to rebel, but in vain. The Committee have solemnly pointed out to such free-thinking and independent spirits that their fathers and grandfathers got on quite well without smoking pipes in the club, and that if their fathers and their grandfathers did without pipes, they ought to be able to do without pipes too—in the club. Oh, yes, they were at liberty, if they liked, to smoke cigarettes at five a penny all over the house, but never tobacco in a pipe, even if they paid half-a-crown an ounce for it.

The conversation of the only two occupants of the smoking-room—try as I would, I could not help listening to it—wearied me so intensely that I got up at last and went out. I strolled aimlessly up the street to Piccadilly, then turned to the left. Many thoughts filled my mind as I rambled along, and when, presently, I found myself at Hyde Park Corner, I decided I would stroll down into Belgravia and see if a new caretaker had been installed at the house in Belgrave Street in place of poor old Taylor.

To my surprise the house was boarded up. Nearly every window was boarded, even the top-floor windows. It looked like a house in which people have died of some plague.

I found the policeman on the beat, and questioned him. Inclined at first to be sullen and uncommunicative, he became cordial and confidential soon after my fingers had slipped a coin into his hand.

"So you haven't heard anything about number a hundred and two," he said some moments later. "About here it's causin' a bit o' talk."

"Indeed? In what way?"

He paused, as though reflecting whether he ought to tell me.

"Well, sir, it's like this," he said at last. "The 'ouse is, as you've seen, boarded up, and there's nobody living there but—"

"Yes? But what?"

"Well, for the last eight nights there's been a light in a window on the first floor."

"A light? But how could you see a light if there were one, with the windows boarded up?"

"Oh, it can be seen right enough, through the chinks between the boards."

"Who has seen it?"

"I have—and others also."

"Is it always in the same window?"

"Not always in the same window, but always on the same floor. Ah, no! On two nights there was a light on the second floor too."

"And at what time is it seen?"

"Very late—not before two in the morning, as a rule."

"And how long does it remain?"

"Sometimes for five or ten minutes, sometimes as much as half-an-hour, or more. Three nights ago two windows were lit up at one-twenty and remained lit until two-fifty-five."

"And do you mean to say nobody goes into the house or comes out of it?"

"Nobody. Nobody at all. It's being watched front and back. Twice we've been in and hunted the place all over—we got leave to do this—but there was nothing, nor no one nowhere."

"Oh," I exclaimed incredulously, "that is a ridiculous thing to say. If a light really appears and disappears, there must be somebody in the house. Probably there's a secret entrance of which you know nothing about."

"There are only three entrances," he answered quickly, "and one of 'em can't rightly be called an entrance. There's the front door, and the back door for the tradesmen, and then there's a queer little way out into Crane's alley—we can't think why that entrance was ever made."

The "queer little way out" I at once guessed to be the dark, underground, narrow little stone cellar-passage through which Vera had led me when we had escaped together on the day I had discovered her hidden in the house.

"And are the entrances all locked?" I asked.

"Oh, you may take that from me," he replied. "They are locked right enough, and nobody don't get the keys, neither."

At that moment, oddly enough, the thought of the curious-looking brown stain in the corner of the ceiling on the first floor, that I had noticed on the day I had explored the unoccupied house, came suddenly back into my mind.

I must have talked to the policeman for fully fifteen minutes, and had asked him many questions. Before the end of that time I had, however, discovered that he was of a superstitious nature, and that he did not at all like what was happening.

I pondered for a little while, then I said—

"Look here, officer"—if you want to please a policeman always call him "officer"—"I am going to peep into that room, and you must help me."

"Me, sir?"

"Yes, you. What are policemen for, except to help people? Now listen. I can't, of course, get into the house, but I am going to arrange for a ladder to be brought here to-night that will reach to the first-floor windows. This street is, I'm sure, quite deserted in the small hours of the morning. The ladder will be hoisted up by the men who bring it, you will keep an eye up and down the street to see that nobody comes along to interrupt us. Then I shall crawl up the ladder and peer in at the window. If there is space between the boards wide enough to admit light, the space must be wide enough to enable me to peep into the room."

"It's a bit risky, sir."

"Risky? Not the slightest. I'll make it worth your while to undertake what risk there is. So that is understood. You are on duty here to-night at two o'clock?"

"Oh, yes, sir, but—"

"There is no 'but.' I shall see you later, then."

I returned to King Street. My man John had a friend who worked for a builder, he told me. This friend of his would, he said, arrange everything, and be delighted to. Oh, yes, he had a ladder. He had several ladders. He could bring along single-handed, a ladder the length I wanted, and set it in position.

This was satisfactory. I went to a theatre in order to kill time, for I felt excited and terribly impatient. I had not told Vera of my plan, or Faulkner, or indeed anybody but the policeman.

The builder's man was punctual to the minute. He had concealed the ladder in Crane's Court before dark, thinking suspicion might be aroused were he to be seen carrying a ladder through the streets of London in the middle of the night. Two o'clock had just struck, when he crept stealthily into Belgrave Square with the ladder over his shoulder. Acting upon my instructions, he laid it flat upon the pavement. Impatiently I waited. A quarter-past two chimed on some far-distant clock. Still the windows remained in darkness.

Twenty minutes passed... Twenty-five... I began to feel anxious. Would this mysterious visitor not come to-night? That would indeed be a bitter disappointment. Ah!

The light had appeared. It was on the first floor. Now it percolated feebly between the boards covering two windows.

At a signal from me the man picked up the ladder, raised it to a vertical position, then let it rest, without a sound, against the window-sill.

"All right, sir," he whispered to me.

Restraining my excitement, I began slowly, cautiously, to creep up the rungs.

Chapter Twenty One.

Contains a Further Surprise.

The boards covering the windows were about an inch thick, but, with the slovenliness unfortunately too common among British workmen, they had been nailed up "anyhow," and between the two boards immediately facing me was a space an inch or more. Through that, I saw the weak light, as of a candle.

Two rungs higher up I climbed, leant forward, and endeavoured to glue my eye to this crack, in order to peer into the room.

It was by no means easy to see more than a narrow strip of the room, and that strip was empty. Guessing, however, that something I should be able to see must soon happen in the room, I decided to wait. I suppose I must have waited about five minutes—it seemed like a quarter of an hour—my eye was beginning to ache, and I had a crick in my neck, when of a sudden a shadow fell across the bare boards—the strip of floor that I could see—and then a second shadow. A moment later a man stood in the room, his back to the window, a light in his hand. At once I recognised the man by his colossal stature.

It was the dark giant I knew as Davies.

What was he doing? I could not see. Some one was beside him, also with his back turned. I started. This second man was Sir Charles Thorold, undoubtedly. They were conversing, but I could not, of course, catch their words.

Sir Charles was bending down. He seemed to be on all fours. Now Davies was on all fours too. They were both crawling on all fours about the floor, as though searching for something.

With breathless interest I watched them. They had passed out of my range of vision, though a pair of feet were still visible. The feet remained in sight for quite a long time, ten minutes or more. Then they too disappeared.

"What on earth are they about?" was my mental comment. "What can they be seeking?"

It had seemed obvious that they had been trying to find something.

Still on the ladder I waited, hoping that something more might happen, but I saw nothing more, and presently the light was extinguished. I judged that some one had carried the candle into another room. Apparently there was no object in waiting longer on the ladder, so I cautiously descended to the ground again.

I felt satisfied, and yet dissatisfied, with the result of my observation.

It was satisfactory to know who the people were who visited the house in this mysterious way in the small hours. But it was unsatisfactory not to have found out why they went there at that time of night, and thus secretively—or why they went there at all.

Just as I reached the ground, thought of the advertisement I had noticed in the *Morning Post* floated back into my mind—

"*Meet me 2.*"

Could there be any connexion between that advertisement and these mysterious visits at two in the morning? It seemed unlikely, and yet it was somewhat curious.

I did not tell the expectant constable more than I deemed it good that he should know. I told him I thought I had discovered the presence of two men in the house, but I did not say they were men I knew and could identify.

He was pleased with the half-sovereign I gave him, and hinted clearly that he would always be glad to render me any service in his power. It always interests me to observe how readily the milk of human kindness comes oozing out where one least expects it, provided the "source" whence it springs is "handled" in the right way.

As he had said this, I determined to take him at his word. I had seen enough to excite my curiosity and to stimulate in me a keen desire actually to enter the house. But how could this be arranged?

Everything is possible of accomplishment, I find, if you set about it in the right way. I had obtained from the policeman his private address in Rodney Street, Walworth Road, and, on the following evening, when he was off duty, I looked in to see him.

Rarely have I been more welcomed by anybody than I was by that policeman and his wife, or more hospitably entertained. Plenty of men of about my own social standing would, I know, think me quite mad if I told them I had hobnobbed with "a common policeman." The club would have been shocked. "My dear fellah," I can hear them saying, "you really should draw the line somewhere, don't you know. A gentleman is a gentleman, and a policeman is—well, is a policeman—eh, what? He may be an exceedingly good and honest fellah, and all that sort of thing, don't you know, but, after all, we must keep to people in our own station of life, or we shall be dining with each other's valets next, and one's friend's butler will be asking one to lunch with him at his club. I'm cosmopolitan myself, up to a point, but really one must keep the classes distinct, we must keep ourselves aloof from the common people, or where will it end, don't you know? As I say, a gentleman is a gentleman, and a man who isn't a gentleman, well, he isn't a gentleman—you can't get away from that."

To which my only reply would be that, to my knowledge, there are plenty of "gentlemen" who are not gentlemen, and quite a sensible proportion of the men we do self-complacently term "bounders" who are men of high ideals and of great refinement.

During supper, to which he had asked me half-apologetically, the constable entertained me with many good stories, for he had been seventeen years in the Metropolitan Police, and had seen much of life in London during that time. I waited until we had finished supper, and his wife had retired, before submitting for his approval the proposal I had come to make.

Mine was quite a simple proposal, though not devoid of risk, yet the plan could not well be carried out without his help. Briefly, I was determined to force an entrance to the house in Belgrave Street on the following night, and the way I had decided to get in was through the dark cellar-passage which opened on to Crane's Alley.

During the afternoon I had visited the Alley, and examined the lock of the gate at the end of the iron railings which topped the wall of the little yard, also the lock of the small door that led into the black cellar-passage which ultimately led into the house. Both, I saw, could easily be forced. Indeed, there would be no need to force the lock of the iron gate. I could climb over the gate, as I had done that day. All this I told the constable, and he calmly nodded.

"And you want me to abet you in this crime," he said at last, with a grin, as he loaded his pipe anew.

"I do," I said. "And—I'll make it worth your while."

"Well, it's house-breaking, you know," he observed drily, filling the room with clouds of smoke. "And you know what the sentence for breaking into a house at night is?"

"Never mind about the sentence," I answered quickly. "I shall have to serve that—and not you! But there won't be any sentence, because there won't be any capture—if you help me. And you are going to help me. Oh, yes, you are."

We both laughed.

"You are a one, sir—an' no mistake!" he exclaimed. "Well, yes, I'll do me best and charnce it. I'm a bit of a sport meself when they gives me arf a charnce."

And so it was settled. It was this policeman's duty to keep an eye on Crane's Alley, which was included in his beat. Well, he would for once forget to keep an eye on it, while the sergeant was out of the way. More, he would lend a hand when the time came to force the lock of the door in the little yard. After that he would be at liberty to slip back to Belgrave Street and resume his monotonous tramp.

And all this would happen on the following night, or rather, about two o'clock next morning.

When I left him it was nine o'clock, and, feeling in high spirits, I drove to the *Grand* to tell Vera my plan, for I felt I must tell somebody. She was alone in the private sitting-room overlooking the thousand lights of Trafalgar Square, and I sat with my arm about her.

"It is madness—sheer madness," she exclaimed, when I had outlined my scheme, "and if you will take my advice—you know my advice is generally sound—you will at once abandon the idea, Dick. It is very well for you to say that my father is your friend, but you don't know my father—you don't know him as I know him. There are two sides to his character. Indeed, I would say he is really two men in one. The man you know is very different from the other man—my father as you have never seen him, and as I hope you never will see him. He can become perfectly savage. He has a temper that is altogether unmanageable when once it gets the better of him. It doesn't often, but when it does—

"No, don't do it, dear, don't, I beg of you. I ask you not to. I beg you not to if you really love me."

"I must," I answered, with a firmness that surprised her. "I have gone too far now to draw back, even if I wanted to, which I don't. I am going to see this thing through. I'm going to discover the mystery of that house. I don't care what risks I take, or what happens, but I am going to see for myself what all this secret business means."

To my surprise she began to laugh.

"Dick," she said, "I sometimes wonder if you are quite 'all there.' Why on earth can't you let people alone, and mind your own business? Supposing Whichelo should turn upon you—good Heavens, he could squeeze the life out of you with one hand."

"Whichelo?" I asked, puzzled, still holding her soft hand in mine.

"Yes. You said when you looked in at the window you saw Whichelo with my father."

Instantly I put two and two together. So the big, dark giant whom I had known only as Davies was called Whichelo!

At last I had found out!

"And why should this man with the funny name, this Whichelo, want to 'squeeze the life out of me' as you so picturesquely put it?" I inquired carelessly, rising and crossing to the window, the blinds of which were not drawn.

"For the simple reason," she answered, "that of course he won't allow you to reveal the secret that has been kept so well, and so long. He and my father would stick at nothing to prevent that—believe me. I tell you again, I know my father."

Somehow, though she spoke calmly, I felt she had some very strong incentive for not wanting me to enter the house and see what was happening there. She seemed to dread my carrying out my plan. Yet apparently she was not anxious on my account. But my mind was now made up. Nothing, I was determined, should stop me. I believed that I was on the eve of making discoveries which would lead to the unravelling of the mystery of Houghton Park, and the mysteries which had followed.

"Good-night, darling," I said, going back to her. I took her in my arms and kissed her. As I did so, I thought I felt her sob.

"Why, Vera, what is the matter?" I exclaimed, releasing her.

"The matter?" she said, forcing a smile. "Nothing. Oh! nothing at all, dear. Why?"

"You—you seemed worried."

"Oh, you're mistaken. Why should I be?" She gave vent to a little hysterical laugh. I kissed her again, and told her to "cheer up." Then I left her. I did not dare trust myself longer in her presence, lest she should, after all, persuade me to change my mind.

Chapter Twenty Two.

A Secret is Disclosed.

The night was still—clear and starlit.

Between two and three in the morning is the one hour when, in London, the very houses seem to slumber, save in a few districts, such as Fleet Street, Covent Garden and its purlieus, where night and day are alike—equally active, equally feverish—those streets which never sleep.

I wore an old suit, a golf cap, shoes with rubber soles, and in my jacket-pocket carried an electric torch. I had decided not to take a pistol. After all, I was not bent on mischief. Also I was going, as I supposed, among friends. Even if Sir Charles were to turn upon me I could not believe he would do me an injury, in spite of my beloved's warning. He and I had known each other such a long time.

Vera, finding that nothing would dissuade me, had ended by giving me the bunch of keys which I had forgotten she still possessed—the keys I had taken from old Taylor's pocket. "If you are determined to do this mad thing, Dick," she had said to me, kissing me fondly, "you may as well get in with the key, instead of house-breaking." On the bunch were the key which would unlock the iron gate, and the one of the little door. This greatly simplified matters, for there were no bolts on the little door, as there were upon the front door and on the tradesmen's door.

The light appeared in the same window on the first floor at exactly twenty minutes past two. Standing in Belgrave Street with my constable friend, who was now on duty, I saw it flicker suddenly. Without further delay we both went round Crane's Alley. Nobody was about. Not a sound anywhere. Noiselessly I unlocked the iron gate, then the little door...

"Good luck, sir," the policeman whispered, as I crept into the dark, low-roofed passage. "And if you want any help, remember you've got the whistle."

There were two little stone-walled cellar-passages, and I took the one to the right. Before I had gone a yard I uttered an exclamation. I was up against a great veil of grey cobwebs which hung from everywhere and was stretched right across the stone passage. So thick were they that I had to push into them to make my way along. How I regretted I had not brought a stick! Suddenly something damp creepy, large, horrible, ran across my face, then another, and another.

Ugh! My blood ran cold at their touch, for I hate spiders.

I pulled out my electric torch. Its sudden glare sent scores of spiders scurrying in all directions. I could actually hear them—nay, I could smell them, and, wherever I looked, I could see them. The sight made me shudder, for they were not, apparently, house-spiders of the usual variety—but large, fat, oval-bodied things, with curved legs, and with protruding heads that seemed to look at me. Indeed, I don't think that in the whole of my life I have ever spent moments that I less like to dwell upon than the two minutes it took me to push my way through that loathsome tangle of evil-smelling cobwebs alive with spiders. I would not go through such an experience again for any sum.

At last I got through them, and I recollect thinking, as I emerged, how foolish I had been to take the wrong turning.

Of course, when Vera had led me out we must have come by the other passage, as there had been no cobwebs then. And that led me further to wonder whether at that time the passage had not been in regular use by some person or persons. I did not for a moment believe that old Taylor had been so conscientious as to keep either passage free of cobwebs, seeing how utterly neglected had been the rest of the house.

In the servants' quarters, where I presently found myself, I recognised at once that same acrid smell of dry rot I had noticed when last in the house, only now it was more "pronounced." Noiselessly I crept along, in my rubber shoes, to the hall. Everywhere the deathly stillness was so intense that one seemed almost to feel it. Cautiously I crept up the front stairs, keeping close to the wall in order to prevent their creaking. My electric torch proved most useful.

I was outside the door of the drawing-room that overlooked Belgrave Street—the first room I had entered on that previous occasion—the room into which I had peered the night before, as I stood upon the ladder. A tiny ray of faint light percolated through the keyhole. I listened, hardly breathing, but could hear no sound at all, except my own heart-beats.

Should I turn the handle gently, slowly push the door ajar, and peep in? It might squeak. Should I fling open the door and rush in? Faced with a problem, I was undecided. I admit that at that moment I felt inclined to run away. Instead, I stood motionless, hesitating, frightened at my own temerity. Had I, after all, been wise in disregarding Vera's good advice?

I thought of that curious brown stain I remembered so distinctly upon the ceiling in this very room. It had been in the right hand corner—the corner farthest from me. What was above that corner? Ah, I knew just where that spot would be in the room above.

Suddenly an idea struck me. I would creep up to the next floor and enter the room above. I had taken from the bunch about eight keys I thought might prove of use. Vera had told me which they were. All were loose in different pockets, each with a tag tied to it, bearing the name of the room it belonged to.

The room upstairs was in darkness, but the door of it was not locked. Cautiously I entered, pushed to the door behind me, and then pressed the button of my electric torch.

Everything was in disorder. Most of the dusty furniture had been pushed into a corner. Some of it was still covered with sheets, but much of it was not. Clearly people had been in here a good deal of late. I picked my way between various pieces of furniture across to the corner I sought. On arriving there I started, and at once switched off my light.

In the floor at that corner, was a big hole, a very big hole indeed, several feet across.

The carpet had been rolled back. The boards had all been ripped up. Two of the beams below them had been sawed across, and about three feet of each of these beams removed. The ceiling of the room below had been smashed away—this I judged to be the exact spot where the brown stain had been—and, as I cautiously bent forward, and craned my neck, I could see right down into the drawing-room.

Voices were murmuring—men's voices. The sight upon which my gaze rested made me recoil.

Stretched out on the floor, right below me, was a human body—shrivelled, dry, quite brown, but undoubtedly a body. It looked exactly like a mummy, a mummy five feet or more in length. Beside it knelt two figures. As I looked, I saw them slowly lift the body from the floor, one man holding either end of it. In a moment or two they had carried it out of sight. And the men who had taken it away were Sir Charles Thorold and the man I had known as Davies, but whose name I now knew to be Whichelo.

This was more, a great deal more than I had expected or even dreamt I should see when I entered the house of mystery.

What could it all mean? Had there been foul play? And if so, had Thorold had a hand in it? I could not think this possible. And yet what other construction could I possibly place upon what I had just witnessed?

I did not know what to think, much less had I any idea of what I ought now to do. And then, all at once, an inspiration came to me.

I took several long breaths. Then, setting my voice at a low, unnatural pitch, I gave vent to a deep, long-drawn-out wail, gradually raising my voice until it ended in a weird shriek.

The stillness below became intense. I paused for perhaps half-a-minute. Then I slowly repeated the wail, ending this time in a kind of unearthly yell.

I knew I had achieved my purpose—knew that the men below were terrified, panic-stricken. I could picture them kneeling beside the shrivelled corpse, literally petrified by horror, their eyes starting from their sockets, their faces bloodless.

Then I walked with measured tread about the floor, the dull "plunk plunk" of my rubber soles sounding, in the depth of the night, and in the stillness of that unoccupied house—ghostly even to me. Next I began to push the furniture about, and a moment later I slammed the door.

There was a wild, a frantic stampede. Both men had sprung to their feet and were dashing headlong down the stairs. I pursued them in the darkness! They heard the quick patter of my rubber shoes upon the stairs behind them, and it seemed to give them wings. Furniture was knocked spinning in the darkness. A terrific crash echoed through the house as, in their blind rush, they hurled on to the stone floor of the hall a big china vase the height of a man which had stood upon a pedestal. A door slammed. Then another, more faintly, a long way down some corridor.

Then once more all was still.

Chuckling at the grim humour of the situation, I went slowly up the stairs again. There was still a light in the first-floor room. I pushed the door open and walked boldly in.

I halted, surprise had petrified me.

The sight that my eyes rested upon I shall not forget as long as ever I live!

Chapter Twenty Three.

Contains Another Revelation.

I stood still in horror, my eyes riveted upon the shrivelled human body. It was stretched out upon several chairs placed side by side. The sight was most gruesome.

Near it, upon the floor, was an ordinary packing-case, in the bottom of which a quantity of wood shavings had been pressed down, to form a sort of bed. At once I realised that this box had been prepared for the reception of the body.

It was about to be smuggled out of the house!

But how did it come to be there? Whose body was it? How long had it been dead? And how had the man—for I saw it was the body of a man, apparently a man of middle-age—come by his death?

It was not the sight of the Thing that had startled me, however, for I had expected to see it there.

What had taken my breath away had been the sight of great heaps of coin upon the floor, gold coin which had evidently just been emptied out of the little sacks close by. Near by were some glass bottles containing powdered metal, some bottles of coloured fluid, and various implements—a couple of metal moulds, a ladle, a miniature hand-lathe, several files, and some curiously-fashioned tools which I judged must be finishing tools used in the manufacture of coin.

The truth was plain—a ghastly unexpected truth.

Thorold and Whichelo were, or had been, in some way concerned in issuing base coin, though to me it seemed hardly possible that Sir Charles could actually be implicated. I picked up a handful of the shining coins, and let them fall between my fingers in a golden stream. If they were not golden French louis they were certainly fine imitations. All the coins were French twenty and ten-franc pieces, I noticed. There were no British coins among them, nor were there coins of any other nation. In all, there must have been several thousands of them.

When I had recovered from my surprise, I began to examine the body more closely. With my electric torch I ran a flash all along it and to and fro. It was the body of a man about thirty, I definitely decided, and it was swathed in brown rags. I had seen bodies in the catacombs in Rome and in Paris that looked like this, and also in South America I had seen some.

South America! My thought of that continent set up a fresh train of thought in my mind. It made me think of Mexico, and the thought of Mexico, though not in South America, brought the tall, dark man, Whichelo, back to me vividly. He had been in Mexico a great deal at one time, Vera had told me. And this mummified body lying in front of me—yes, it singularly resembled the mummified bodies I had seen in Mexico when on my travels about the world.

What had caused death? Critical inspection with my electric torch showed distinctly a fracture at the base of the skull, as though it had been struck with some blunt implement, such as a hammer.

Yes, there could be no doubt that the skull had been severely fractured. I should have held the theory that the poor fellow had been attacked from behind, felled to the ground with some iron weapon. I wondered greatly how long the man had been dead. No expert knowledge was needed to decide that he must have been dead a number of years. And where had the body been hidden all this time?

Instinctively I glanced at the ceiling—at the gaping hole in it—and instantly I knew. This mummified body had been hidden away, buried between the ceiling and floor! It had been in that corner, where the hole now was. And the brown stain I had noticed in the corner of the ceiling...

But the money? Why, of course, the money must have been there, too. A thought struck me. I picked up some of the coins again, and glanced at the dates. Twenty-five or thirty years ago they were dated, yet they looked quite new. Clearly, then, they had not been in circulation. Paulton's significant remark returned to me—the remark he had made that night in the room in Château d'Uzerche, when I had said something about not revealing Sir Charles Thorold's secret.

Could there be some hidden connexion between this discovery I had made, Thorold's secret, and the charge upon which Paulton was "wanted?"

I spent some time in examining the room and its contents. Then I explored other parts of the house.

Was I now gradually approaching the solution of Sir Charles Thorold's secret?

I believed it more than likely that I might now at last be well on my way to solving the mystery of Houghton Park and the Thorolds' sudden flight. That Sir Charles and his big friend would not return that night I fully believed. They might, or might not, be superstitious, but there could be no doubt I had terrified them thoroughly. If they returned at all it would be in the daytime, I conjectured.

What was to be done? How should I act?

I decided that the only thing to do would be to go out into the street and inform the constable of all that had happened. I had told him I would not stay long in the house in any case, and my prolonged absence might be making him feel uneasy.

I left by the front door—which I found securely bolted and chained on the inside—and there found the constable flashing his bull's-eye lantern upon the door, and with his truncheon ready drawn.

"Hush!" I whispered, and he smiled upon seeing me, and at once replaced his truncheon.

"I was beginning to feel very anxious on your account, sir," he said. "I 'arf wondered who might be a-comin' out. Well, sir, did you see anything?"

"I should say so," I answered, and then, as briefly as I could, I told him nearly everything.

I persuaded him to come in then and there.

"Well, look at that, now!" he said, as I showed him first the mummified body, then the sacks of gold, and pointed out to him the great hole cut in the ceiling. "Well, look at that, now!" he repeated.

"The awkward part of the affair is this," I said at last. "Who is going to lodge information? I don't care to, for, if I do, inquiries will be made as to how I came to be on the premises at all, and how I managed to get in, and it won't look well if I am proved, on my own showing, to have entered the place secretly in the middle of the night. Again, I don't want to lodge information against Sir Charles Thorold. Why should I? He has always been my friend. Nor, for that matter, do I want to prefer any sort of charge against Whichelo. So far as the body is concerned, we may be quite wrong in conjecturing that there has been foul play. Indeed, there is no actual proof that the mummy was hidden in the ceiling of the room, though personally I think it must have been. Everything points to it. And you, Bennett, can't very well give information either without compromising yourself as well as me. Your inspector would want to know how you managed to get into the house, and what right you had to enter it."

I paused, considering, while he removed his helmet and scratched his head.

"I'll tell you what I think we had better do," I said at last.

"Well, sir, what?" he inquired eagerly.

"Nothing. Nothing at all. Go back to your beat. I'll bolt and chain the front door when you're gone. Then I'll put out the light in this room, and make my way out of the house by the way I entered it."

"But the two men," the policeman said quickly. "Where can they have got to? They can't have left the premises."

"You may depend upon it they have," I answered. "I feel pretty sure there must be some secret entrance to this house, that they alone know. The back door, too, is bolted and chained on the inside, and they can hardly have entered the way I did—ugh!" and I shuddered again at the thought of those horrible, hairy-legged spiders scampering over my bare flesh.

"*Meet me 2.*"

Again that odd little advertisement arose in my thoughts. I would watch the front page of the *Morning Post* for a day or two. Perhaps another advertisement might appear that would help me.

Early next day I went and told Vera everything. I found her seated in the lounge on the right of the hall.

She listened eagerly, and I saw at once that the news excited her a good deal, yet to my surprise she made no comment, but changed the subject of conversation by remarking—

"Violet brought Frank Faulkner here yesterday evening. He is engaged to be married to her. He has broken off his engagement to Gladys Deroxe, and I am very glad he has," she declared.

"Really," I exclaimed. "Well, frankly I'm not surprised, for I believe he has been in love with Violet from the moment he first met her. But how did Miss Deroxe take it? Was there a dreadful scene?"

"Scene? There was no scene at all, it appears. What happened was simply this. Gladys discovered that Frank had brought Violet over from the Riviera, that she was staying here at his expense, and that he seemed to be extremely attentive to her. Now, a sensible girl would have asked her future husband, in a case of that sort, to come to see her and explain everything. That, certainly, is what I should have done."

"And what did Miss Deroxe do?"

"Do? Good Heavens, she sat down then and there and wrote him a letter—oh! such a letter! He showed it to me. I have never in my life read anything so insulting. She ended by telling him in writing that she had never really cared for him, and that she hoped she would never see him again. In one place she wrote: 'I might have guessed the kind of man you are by the kind of company you keep. I know all about your friend, Richard Ashton. He associates with dreadful people. I am only glad I have found you out before it was too late!' Those were her words. So you see the kind of reputation you have acquired, my dear Dick."

I laughed—laughed uproariously. I, "the associate of dreadful people," I, a member of that hot-bed of conventions and of respectability, Brooks's Club. The whole thing was delicious.

"When will Frank and Violet be here again?"

I asked presently, after we had ascended together to the private sitting-room.

"I've invited Frank to lunch. I told them you were coming. Frank has something important to tell you, he said."

"Did he tell you what?"

"No. At least it had reference, he said, to the Château d'Uzerche, or to something that has been found there. To tell the truth, I was thinking of something else when he told me."

"Dearest," I said, some minutes later, my arm about her waist, "you remember my telling you I had taken a few of the coins I found in your father's house. Well, yesterday I had them tested. They are not counterfeits. They are genuine."

She looked at me curiously. Then, after a pause, she said—

"What made you think they might be counterfeit?"

"What made me think so? Seeing that I discovered with them a number of implements, etc, used apparently in the manufacture of base coin, my inference naturally was that the coins must have been false."

Still she looked at me. Gradually her expression hardened.

"Dick," she said at last, "you are deceiving me. You have deceived me all along. You told me you knew my father's secret. Now you don't know it—do you?"

"Indeed you are mistaken, quite mistaken, dearest," I exclaimed quickly. "I know it well enough, but I don't, I admit, know that part of it which bears upon these coins. I never pretended to know that part."

It was a wild shot, but I felt I must say something in my defence.

I hated deceiving Vera in this way, as, indeed, I should have hated to deceive her in any way, but, playing a part still, I was driven to subterfuge. After all, I had never said I knew her father's secret. She had jumped to the conclusion that I knew it, that day I had found her locked in the upper room in the house in Belgrave Street, and I had not disillusioned her. That was all.

The door of the sitting-room opened at that moment, we sprang apart as Faulkner and Violet entered. The pretty girl, in a blue serge coat and skirt, looked radiantly happy, and the happiness she felt seemed to increase her great beauty. I confess I had not before fully realised what a lovely girl she was.

"Ah, Dick, my dear fellow," Faulkner exclaimed, grasping me by the hand, "I want you to congratulate me, old chap."

"Oh, I do, of course," I said at once. "I congratulate you doubly—on becoming engaged, and on breaking off your engagement."

He made a quick little gesture of impatience.

"Oh, I don't mean congratulations of that kind," he said quickly. "I shouldn't ask you to waste your time in congratulating me upon anything so commonplace as an engagement of marriage. I want you to congratulate me upon something you don't yet know."

"Well, what is it?" I said impatiently. "Have you come into a fortune?"

"Right the very first time!" he exclaimed. "Yes, I have. I've inherited, quite unexpectedly, a very large fortune. But the odd thing is this. My benefactor is, or rather was, unknown to me. Until yesterday I had never even heard his name."

"How wonderful! But how splendid!" I cried out. "Do tell me more about it. Tell me everything."

"I will. And now prepare to receive a shock. The will leaving me this fortune was found in the safe discovered among the débris of Château d'Uzerche, after the fire?"

Chapter Twenty Four.

A Further Tangle.

Certainly, this was a most remarkable development. I listened without comment.

Yet when Faulkner had given me, at the luncheon table, all the details by way of "explanation," as he put it, the tangle seemed even greater than before he had begun.

The will, dated three years previously, had been drawn up by a well-known firm of London lawyers. It was quite in order, and the testator's name was Whichelo, Samuel Whichelo, formerly of Mexico City, merchant, but then resident at Wimbledon Common. The testator, who had been unmarried, left a few legacies to friends and servants, but practically the whole of his fortune he bequeathed entirely to Frank Faulkner, "in return for the considerable service he once rendered me."

Faulkner had handed me a copy of the will—it was quite a short will. When I came to this sentence I naturally looked up.

"Ah!" I said, "then there is a method in the testator's madness. But I thought you told me you had never even heard his name."

"Until yesterday I never had heard it."

"Then what was this 'considerable service' he says you rendered him?"

"Well, I'll tell you," he said. "Years ago, when I was knocking about the world—I was then about twenty—I chanced to find myself, one night, in the China Town of San Francisco. I had a friend with me, about my own age. Foolishly, we were exploring at night, alone—that is, without an interpreter or guide of any sort, which is about as risky a thing as any ordinary unarmed European can do in San Francisco, where you may still, I believe, find the scum of all the nations. Suddenly we heard a cry. A man was calling, '*Au secours! Au secours!*' Without stopping to think, I rushed in the direction whence the cry came. It was repeated. It was in a house which I recognised, at a glance, as an establishment of doubtful repute. I must tell you that when I was twenty I was considered a first-rate boxer, and it may have been the confidence I felt in my ability to defend myself that made me rush, without hesitation, into that Chinese den. Cards and chits were scattered about the tables and on the floor, and nine or ten Chinamen were in the room, struggling furiously with a tall, dark man of powerful build, who was being rapidly overcome owing to the number of his assailants. Chinese oaths were flying about freely, and I saw a knife-blade flash suddenly into the air."

He paused for a second, then continued—

"My blood was up. I felt as I feel sometimes now, that I didn't care for anything or any one or what might happen to me. I rushed at the nearest Chinaman like a maniac—I believe he thought I was one. My first blow knocked him silly. Then, right and left I hit out. I was in perfect condition at that time. Down went the Chinamen one after another, as my blows caught them on the chin—I used to be famous for that chin-blow, I 'specialised' in it, so to speak. I detest boasting. I tell this only to you, because I think it may amuse you and explain my windfall. In less than two minutes I had stretched five of the Chinamen senseless with that chin-blow, and the remaining three or four, seized with panic, fled."

"What then?" I asked.

"At once I led the man who had called for help out into the street. I saw he was pretty badly hurt, so with the help of my friend, who had now joined me again, I got him out of China Town, expecting to be set upon at any moment by friends of those Chinamen, thirsting for revenge. Though he had called '*Au secours*!' he was not French, it seemed. He was British Portuguese, though he lived in Mexico, he told me later. We got him to the hospital. 'I must have your name—I must have your name,' he exclaimed quite excitedly, as I was leaving, I remember. 'You have rendered me a service I shall never forget—never. You must come and see me to-morrow.' I told him I could not do that, as I was leaving early next morning for Raymund, on my way to the Yosemite Valley. But I said I hoped we might meet again some day, and, as he insisted upon my doing so, I gave him a card with my address—my London club address. It was at the club that I found, yesterday morning, the communication from his lawyers."

"And by Gad!" I exclaimed enthusiastically, "you deserve this 'bit of luck,' as you call it, Frank. I think you acted splendidly!"

"Oh, for Heaven's sake don't become emotional, old chap," he said hurriedly. "If you knew how I hate gush, you wouldn't."

"It isn't gush," I answered. "What wouldn't I have given to see you buckling up those Chinamen one after another. Splendid!"

I turned to Violet.

"I congratulate you," I said, taking her hand, "on marrying a real man. I think the two of you are the pluckiest pair I have ever met. It will be long before I forget that incident on the roof of Château d'Uzerche. But for you, neither Frank nor I would be alive to-day."

"Nor the Baronne, nor Dago Paulton," she added mischievously. "Oh, yes, I am a heroine! A heroine to save such very precious lives!"

"Are you not grateful to the Baronne?" I asked quickly. "After all, she did adopt you, and bring you up."

"Yes," the girl answered, with a swift, reproachful glance, "she adopted me and brought me up, but only that I might help to further her own ends. She didn't adopt me out of affection, I can assure you."

I saw that I had again trodden upon thin ice, so I quickly changed the topic.

"But the great mystery," I said, addressing Faulkner, "is not yet solved. How on earth did Whichelo's will, leaving you this fortune, come to be in the safe in Château d'Uzerche, in the Basses Alpes? When did Whichelo die?"

"Four months ago. The lawyers distinctly remember him making a will, but he had never returned it to them, and, since his death, they had been trying to find it. They even advertised for it."

"To whom would his fortune have gone, had he died intestate?" I inquired suddenly.

"To his younger brother, Henry. From what the lawyers tell me, this brother of his must be a peculiar man. His life appears to be a mystery. He is, however, known to be intimate with your friend, Sir Charles Thorold. Sir Charles and he were in Mexico together ten years ago, the lawyers tell me, and were there again about three years ago."

"Who are the lawyers who wrote to you?" something prompted me to ask.

"You mean about the will? Oh, a firm in Lincoln's Inn, Spink and Peters."

Instantly I thought of old Taylor.

"Ah," I said, "I have heard of them. Thorold has had some business dealings with them. By the way—who opened the safe?"

"The French police. It seems, that since the fire, neither Dago Paulton nor the Baronne de Coudron have shown any signs of life. Even the insurance people have not been written to by them."

"Paulton and the Baronne are probably afraid of being arrested," I said at once.

We talked a little longer, but Faulkner seemed unable to throw any further light on the mystery of the will being found in the safe, and the lawyers were equally in the dark. Probably they would never have heard of the will had the French police not communicated with them.

"Oh, I have another bit of news for you," Faulkner said suddenly. "Sir Charles Thorold is to return to Houghton."

"My father going back to Houghton!" Vera exclaimed, amazed. "Why, who told you that? I've heard nothing of it."

"Read it in the newspaper this morning," Faulkner answered. "I have the paper here—in my pocket."

He tugged out of his coat-pocket a copy of a morning paper, unfolded it, and presently found the announcement.

"There it is," he said, passing the paper to her, with his finger on the paragraph.

The announcement ran as follows—

"We are able to state that Sir Charles and Lady Thorold have decided to return to their country residence, Houghton Park, in Rutland, which has been vacant since the mysterious affair when the body of Sir Charles' butler was discovered in the lake at Houghton, and the chauffeur from Oakham was shot dead by an unknown assassin. The news is creating considerable interest throughout the county."

"What an astonishing thing!" I exclaimed. "Really, one may cease being surprised at anything. I wonder how 'the county' will receive them. I prophecy that the majority of Rutland society will cut them dead, after what has happened."

"Why should they?" Faulkner asked, in surprise. "There's no reason why they should," I answered "I only say they will. You don't know Rutland county people—or you wouldn't ask."

Vera's lunch-party had proved a great success. The four of us had been in the best of spirits. And yet, once, at least, during the meal, Paulton's face, dark, threatening, floated into my imagination, and again I heard that ominous threat he had uttered in Paris that night, the last words I had heard him speak—

"I shall be even with you soon, in a way you don't expect."

Where was he at this moment? What plot was he hatching? Had he left Paris? Was he in London? Would he and the Baronne try to get Violet away from Faulkner by force?

Though now we were all so light-hearted, I could not help thinking of Paulton and the Baronne, and wondering what their next clever move would be. It was not to be supposed they would remain dormant. They were probably lying "doggo," in order to spring with greater force.

During the same week I looked in again at Rodney Street on my policeman, who expressed himself delighted to see me. Some days had now passed since

I had forced my way into the house in Belgrave Street during the night. I was wondering what had happened there since; whether lights had been seen again; whether anybody else had been into the place; or if the body and the gold had been removed.

When he had pushed forward his most comfortable chair, and I had seated myself in it, the constable said: "I have some news for you to-day, sir."

"News?" I exclaimed. "What kind of news?"

"Well, simply this, sir. All them sacks of money has been removed, but the mummy has been left just where it was. The police have possession of it now."

"When did they take possession of it?" I asked quickly, starting up.

"Yesterday. Mr Spink, in whose hands the house is during Sir Charles Thorold's absence, went there. I see him when he comes out, and I never in my life see a man look so white and scared. He found the body lying there, of course, also all the furniture pushed about, and the great hole cut in the ceiling. When he came out he was as terrible pale, and shivering with excitement. It was about three in the afternoon. He called me at once, and I went in with the man on point-duty. Everything was much as when you and me saw it, sir, only there wasn't no money."

"Then of course Whichelo and Sir Charles have taken it away. I wonder at their leaving the body, though. Such a give-away, isn't it? Did the police find out how the men entered and left the house?"

"I found that out, sir—quite by charnce. There's a way into a cellar we didn't know of, and that cellar leads into the cellar of the house adjoining, which is empty. That's the way they went in and out. It was easy to see as how somebody had been to and fro that way."

"Do the police know anything of the money?" I asked. "Didn't they see any sign of it at all?"

"No, sir. Nor Mr Spink didn't neither."

"Do they suspect who has been into the house?"

"No, sir, they ain't got no idea. And about the body and how it got there, they are quite at sea." Sauntering along Victoria Street, Westminster, half-an-hour later, the thought occurred to me to look in on my doctor, David Agnew, who was also my old personal friend.

For some days I had not been well. A feeling of lassitude had come over me, also loss of appetite. Agnew was generally able to prescribe for my simple ailments.

He was a bright, genial fellow, and merely to meet him seemed to do one good. None would have taken him for the celebrated bacteriologist he was, for I—and I think most people—usually picture a bacteriologist as a cadaverous, ascetic, preternaturally solemn individual, with a bald head, wrinkled brow, and large, gold-rimmed spectacles. It was Thorold who had introduced me to Agnew many years before, and many and many a time had the three of us dined together.

At first I was told that the doctor was "not at home," but upon sending in my card, I was immediately admitted.

The shock I received upon entering Agnew's consulting-room, I am not likely to forget. Instead of the hearty greeting I had expected, I was faced by a man whose staring eyes spoke terror. It was Agnew, but I saw at once that something terrible must have happened.

He was pacing the room with his handkerchief to his mouth when I entered. He turned at once, and came over to me.

"Ashton," he said abruptly, taking my hand in both his own, and gripping it so that I almost cried out, "I have an awful thing to tell you—you are the one man in whom I can confide in this crisis, and I am truly glad you've come. I feel I must tell some one. I shall go mad if I don't."

His expression appalled me.

"What is it? What?" I exclaimed. "For Heaven's sake don't look at me like this!"

"I must tell you, I must," he gasped. "Our mutual, our dear friend, Charles Thorold, was in here an hour ago. I had been called out for five minutes, but he said he would wait. As I had a patient in here, Gregory, my man, showed Thorold into the room upstairs—my laboratory. In an open box on the table were several little glass tubes containing bacilli—different sorts of bacilli that I've been cultivating. It seems that Charles, with fatal curiosity, picked up one of these tubes to examine it. The glass of the tube is very thin. One of them broke in his hand—ah! What catastrophe could be more complete? It's terrible... horrible!" He stopped abruptly, unable to go on.

"Well? Why so terrible! Tell me!" I exclaimed.

He pulled himself together with an effort.

"That tube contained a cultivation of pneumonic plague," he exclaimed huskily, "one of the deadliest microbes known. The blood-serum in which I had grown the germs fell upon his hands. Not suspecting the danger, he actually wiped it off with his handkerchief! I did not return until a quarter of an hour afterwards. The evil was then beyond remedy. He became infected!"

"Phew! What will happen now?"

"Happen? In a few days at most he will be dead! There are no recoveries from pneumonic plague—that most terrible contagious disease so well-known in Eastern Siberia and Japan. There is no hope for him. None. You hear—none!"

"By Gad!" I gasped, horrified. "You can't mean it. Where is Thorold now?"

"In isolation at St. George's hospital. I sent him there at once. Oh! Heaven, it is too terrible to think of—and my fault, all my fault for leaving the tube there!"

I tried to calm him, but he was quite beside himself.

I halted, astounded at the gravity of the situation.

Chapter Twenty Five.

Towards the Truth.

Though I hated to cause pain to Vera, I realised that I must immediately tell her. The thought of breaking the terrible news to her upset me, yet the thing had to be faced.

Never shall I forget those awful moments. I had tried to break the news gently, but how can such tragic news be broken "gently"? That conventional word is surely a mockery when used in such a connexion.

She was devoted to her parents. What seemed to trouble her now more than anything else, was the fact that we did not know her mother's whereabouts, and so could not inform her of the frightful *contretemps*.

"Try not to worry, dearest," I said, placing my hand tenderly upon her shoulder, and kissing her upon the lips in an endeavour to soothe her. "We are bound very soon to find out where she is."

"Yes," she retorted bitterly, "and by that time—by that time poor father may be dead!"

She was silent for a few moments, then she said—

"The only thought that comforts me, dear, a little, is that, if he should die, the living lie will die with him. He is so good, so kind, so self-sacrificing, that I think he would be quite ready to die if he thought his death would relieve us of the fearful tension of these last horrible years. My dear, dear father! Ah, how stormy has his life been! Does he know what you have just told me—I mean, that he cannot live?"

"No," I replied.

She began to weep bitterly again, and I did my best to calm her, and kissed her again. I told her he did not know the danger, which was the truth. Agnew had only told him the germs would probably make him very ill for awhile.

The house-physician at the hospital had not broken the actual truth to him—the truth that, infected with such deadly germs he was doomed to death. Perhaps I ought not to have told Vera the whole ghastly truth. Yet, upon carefully considering the matter, I had decided that frankness would be better.

"I will telephone to St. George's," I said, a little later, "and ask for the latest news. You'd better not go to see him until the house-physician gives you leave. He asked me to tell you that."

The reply was satisfactory. Sir Charles was not in pain, the hall-porter said. He was slightly feverish. That was all. What grim consolation!

Two eager days passed. Still Lady Thorold showed no sign of life. I had telephoned to Messrs Spink and Peters. Also I had telegraphed to Houghton Park, as it was said Lady Thorold intended to return there. But to no purpose. One thing that surprised me was that Whichelo had not been to the hospital. Where was he during these days? Had he, too, not heard of the calamity?

"You have not heard the exciting news," I said to Faulkner, when I met him outside the Devonshire on the way to his club.

"What exciting news?" he inquired, in his cool phlegmatic way. "You get excited so easily, Dick, if you will forgive my saying so."

He listened with interest to the news, and when I had done talking, he said quite calmly—

"Curious to relate, I saw the Baroness, Paulton and Henderson not ten minutes ago."

"Saw them!" I gasped. "Where?"

"In Piccadilly, not thirty yards from here. They turned up Dover Street, and went down in the tube lift."

"Are you positive?"

"Quite. I couldn't well forget them. They were walking together, laughing and chatting as though nothing were amiss. I admire that kind of nerve."

Meanwhile, the newspapers were full of the remarkable discovery of the mummified man in Sir Charles Thorold's house in Belgrave Street. The hole cut in the ceiling gave rise to all sorts of wild surmises.

It did not, however, occur to any of the reporters that the body might have been hidden between the ceiling and the floor.

What the newspapers worried about most was the mummy's age. Experts put their heads together, and put on their spectacles. Some were of the opinion that it must be centuries old. Sir Charles, the one man who might have thrown some light upon it could not, of course, be questioned. Only one medical expert, an old professor, differed from his *confrères*. A wizened little man, himself not unlike a mummy, he maintained, in the face of scientific ridicule, that the mummy found in Belgrave Street had been dead "less than twenty years." Further, he pronounced that the method of embalming was a process uncommon in this country or in Egypt, but still in vogue in China and in Mexico. He believed the body to be, he said, that of a man of middle-age, a Spaniard, or possibly a Mexican.

The news of Sir Charles' condition was more satisfactory that evening, inasmuch as the sister at the hospital told me, when I called, that he was still no worse. Perhaps, after all, Dr Agnew had been mistaken. Oh, how I hoped he had been, for my own sake, almost as much as for my darling's.

"I think," I said to Vera, whose spirits rose a little when she heard my report, "that to-morrow morning I will run down to Oakham, to have another look at Houghton."

"What on earth for?" she exclaimed, in a tone of surprise. "I intended asking father to-day, when I saw him at the hospital, if the report that he intended returning to Houghton were true. He seemed so hot and restless however, that I decided not to ask him until to-morrow. I do believe he is going to get better, don't you? But now, tell me what good do you think you will do by going out to Houghton?"

"Good?" I answered. "I don't expect or intend to do good. No, it is merely that something—I can't tell you what—prompts me to go again to see the place."

"How silly!" Vera declared, as I thought rather rudely. Modern girls are so dreadfully outspoken. I do sometimes wish we were back in the days when a matron would raise her hands in dismay and exclaim: "Oh, fie!" or "Oh, la!" when a young girl did aught that seemed to her "unladylike."

Yet, in spite of Vera's remonstrance, I caught a train to Oakham early next morning. Sir Charles had had a restless night, the hospital porter told me on the telephone, before I started, but his condition was surprisingly satisfactory.

Then I rang up Dr Agnew.

"Don't you think he may, after all, recover?" I inquired eagerly.

In reply the doctor said he "only hoped and trusted that he might." More than that, he would not tell me. I gathered, therefore, that he still had serious fears.

I arrived at the *Stag's Head*, in Oakham, in time for lunch. Directly after lunch I started out for Houghton in a hired car.

What a lot had happened, I reflected, as in the same car in which the chauffeur had been shot, we purred down the main street, since I had last set out along that road. What a number of stirring incidents had occurred—incidents crowded into the space of a few weeks. But at last they seemed to be coming to an end. That thought relieved me a good deal. Ah, if only—if only Thorold would recover!

The drive to Houghton from Oakham was a pretty one, past woods and rich grazing pastures until suddenly, turning into the great lodge-gates, we went for nearly a quarter of a mile up the old beech avenue to where stood the old Elizabethan house, a large, rambling pile of stone, so full of historic associations.

On pulling up at the ancient portico, I found to my surprise, the front door ajar. I pushed it open and entered. There was nobody in the big stone hall—how well I remembered the last day when we had all had tea there after hunting, and that fateful message from the butler that "Mr Smithson" had called to see Sir Charles. I made my way into the drawing-rooms, then into the morning-room, and afterwards into the dining-room. The doors were all unlocked, but the rooms were empty. It was while making my way towards the kitchen quarters that I heard footsteps somewhere in the house.

They were coming down the back stairs.

I waited at the foot of the stairs, just out of sight. They were firm, heavy footfalls. A moment later, a tall man stood facing me.

It was the dark giant I had first met at dinner at the *Stag's Head*, when we had shared a table on the night of the Hunt Ball—the man whom I now knew to be Henry Whichelo.

Chapter Twenty Six.

Mr Smithson again.

He gave a hardly perceptible start on seeing me. Then he extended his big hand and grasped mine in the most friendly way.

"Well, this is a real surprise—a very pleasant surprise, Mr Ashton," he said, looking me full in the eyes. "I have often thought of you since the evening we met and had that pleasant meal together, and I told you my name was Smithson, because I knew the name would puzzle you. And what are you doing here? Making an ocular survey—as I am?"

The ready lie rose to my lips. It is very well for moralists to tell us we should always speak the truth. There are occasions when an aptitude for wandering into paths of falsehood may prove extremely useful. It did so now.

"No," I answered, "I'm not. I am on my way to my little place about twenty miles from here—it is let now, but I think of returning to live there—and it occurred to me to look in at Houghton again. I saw it mentioned, in some paper the other day, that the Thorolds are returning."

"Yes, that is so," Whichelo answered. "Sir Charles has instructed me to see to everything, and make all arrangements. I have only to-day heard that he is very ill at the hospital. Have you seen him?"

I told him the latest bulletin. Then I asked him if he had any idea of Lady Thorold's whereabouts.

"All I know," he answered, "is that she was abroad when last I heard of her."

"Abroad? Was that lately?"

"About a week ago. She was then somewhere in the Basses Alpes. Has she not been to see Sir Charles?"

"No. We don't know where she is."

"Who do you mean by 'we'?"

"Vera Thorold and myself."

"That's strange," he said thoughtfully. "Oh, of course Lady Thorold can't have heard of his illness. She would have come at once, or at any rate have telegraphed, if she had."

We talked a little longer—we had strolled into the morning-room, and sat down there—when Whichelo said suddenly—

"That discovery of a mummy in Sir Charles' town house is curious, eh? How would you account for that, Ashton? And for the hole in the ceiling?"

"I don't account for it at all," I replied quickly, trying to look unconcerned beneath his narrow, scrutinising gaze. "What is your theory with regard to it?"

"Oh, I never theorise in cases of that kind," he replied. "What is the use of theorising? One is almost certain to be wrong."

"You must, however," I said with some emphasis, "have some view or other as to the mummy's age. Do you think it is an ancient mummy, or a modern one?"

He smiled, showing his wonderfully white teeth, which contrasted strangely with his crisp, black beard.

"I am not a 'mummy expert,' so I won't venture an opinion," he replied. "I should say the best thing they can do is to bury it, or give it to some museum. I'm sure Thorold won't want it."

"Don't you think," I said, speaking rather slowly, "Thorold may know how it came to be concealed there?"

"What a ridiculous idea, if you will pardon my saying so," Whichelo answered quite sharply. "What on earth can he know about it?"

"After all," I said, in the same even tone, "it was found in his house. Now, I have a theory. Shall I tell you what it is?"

He could not well say "no," though I noticed he was not anxious to listen to the expression of my views or theories on the subject.

"Well," I continued, looking at him steadily, "I have a theory regarding that strange hole in the ceiling. Can you guess what it is?"

"I'm sure I can't," he said, rather uneasily. "What is it?"

"My belief is that the mummy has been for a long time hidden in that ceiling—between the ceiling and the floor above. They lifted the boards of the upper room to get the mummy out, when the ceiling, rotted by decay, fell down. That's my belief. You will, I think, find in the end that I'm right, though the idea does not seem, as yet, to have occurred to anybody else."

Whichelo laughed. It was obviously a forced laugh.

"By Jove! you have a vivid imagination, Ashton," he said, "only I fear you won't find many, if any, to agree with your theory. Why should the mummy have been hidden in the ceiling? Who would have hidden it? People usually have some reason for doing things," he ended, with a touch of malice.

"They have," I answered significantly. Then, unable to resist the impulse, I added with affected carelessness: "I suppose, if a man hid a bag of gold, he would have some reason for hiding it, especially if he hid it in a ceiling. What do you think?"

The man's countenance blanched to the lips. His mouth twitched. He seemed unable to utter a word.

"What do you know?" he suddenly exclaimed hoarsely, clutching the arm of his chair with trembling fingers. Then he added, in a threatening tone: "Tell me!"

I remembered that I was alone with him in there, miles from everywhere. When standing, he towered high above me, a veritable giant, and I knew that, if he chose to attack me, he must overcome me with the greatest ease. At all costs I must pacify him.

"Perhaps now," I said calmly, "you think there is more in my theory than at first appeared. Listen to me, Mr Whichelo," I went on, forcing my courage, "from what I have said, and hinted, you probably guess that I know—well—something. It remains for you to decide whether we are to be friends—or not. Personally, I am willing to be friendly with you. Thorold and I are friends, and have been for years. In addition, I am to marry Vera, so, naturally, I should prefer to remain friendly with her friends. Why not take me into your confidence, and tell me all you know? I'm not a man to talk, I assure you."

I knew I had done right to take him in that way, and to be quite frank with him. Had I shown the white feather at all, even by implication, he would have pounced down upon me. That I felt instinctively.

Our eyes met sharply. During those brief moments something passed between us that revealed our true characters to each other. I had never really mistrusted Whichelo, though on that night we had dined together at the *Stag's Head* in Oakham, his manner and his mode of speech had puzzled me a good deal. Now I instinctively knew him to be a man upon whom I could rely.

"Tell me all you know," he said, in a low tone, glancing about him to make sure we were alone.

At once I came to the point.

"First, I know," I said slowly, "that the body was hidden in the ceiling. Secondly, I believe the old professor's theory which you have probably read in the newspapers, that the mummy has not really been dead very many years. Thirdly, I know that you and Thorold entered that house by way of the cellar of the house adjoining—and I don't mind telling you that it was I who frightened you and Thorold out of your lives by giving vent to that screech in the room above."

"You!" he gasped, surprised.

"Yes, but don't interrupt me," I said. "You and he brought the body to light and intended to smuggle it out of the house in a packing-case."

I stopped. Then, with my eyes still set on his, I said—

"I saw those implements for coining, which afterwards disappeared. More than that—*I saw the bags of gold!*" Then I paused. "What has become of them?" I added meaningly.

Whichelo held his breath.

"By Heaven!" he exclaimed suddenly. "Then you know everything! How did you find this out?"

I made a random shot.

"If you will boldly advertise," I said, "what else can you expect? *'Meet me two.'*"

My shot hit its mark. At once I saw that the advertisement really had reference to the affair.

"Surely," I said, "there was no need to advertise? You could have communicated by post, telegram or telephone!"

"Ah! you are mistaken," he answered quickly. "We had reasons for advertising—but I cannot explain them now. Tell me, knowing all that you know—how you discovered it I don't attempt to guess—but what are you going to do?"

"Do?—Nothing. It's no concern of mine."

"But—but—"

"There is no 'but,'" I interrupted, "except that, having told you what I know, Mr Whichelo, I expect your full confidence in return."

"And you shall have it, Ashton," he exclaimed at once. "Oh, I can assure you, you shall have it."

"Then perhaps you'll tell me first," I said abruptly, "how that will of your brother's came to be found in the safe among the ruins of Château d'Uzerche after the fire. Had it not been found, you would, I understand, have been sole heir to the fortune your brother left to Frank Faulkner."

"Yes, you are quite right," he answered, with a quiet laugh. "I should have been. That will was stolen from my brother."

"So I guessed. But by whom?"

"By Paulton and the Baronne, his companion."

"Stolen by Paulton and the Baronne!" I echoed. "But in what way could they benefit by stealing it, as the money would have come to you had the will not been found? Why did they not destroy it?"

"Well—to tell the truth, they have a hold over me," he went on quickly, "just as they have over Thorold. Probably they refrained from destroying it, intending to get Faulkner into their clutches."

"I don't follow you," I said. "Even if they have a hold over you, as you say, they could not have benefited by you inheriting this money."

"Ah! You are mistaken," he answered. "They would have benefited considerably. Had I inherited that fortune, it must all have gone to them. I can't say more than that."

"Blackmail?" I asked.

He nodded.

"And do they blackmail Thorold in the same way?"

Again he nodded in the affirmative.

At last I seemed to be really on the verge of unravelling the mystery which had puzzled me so long—also on the way to discovering the closely-guarded secret of the Thorolds.

After a brief pause, I put another question to him.

"Is all that French gold I have seen, genuine?" I asked. "I know some of it is, because I had some tested."

"How many?" he inquired, in a tone of surprise.

"Three. They were all good."

"Most of them are base coin," he said. "A small proportion only are coin from the French mint."

"Then Thorold—and you, also, I take it—have had to do with uttering base coin."

"You are wrong—in a sense. It may appear so to you. It would seem so to most people, most likely. In point of fact we are both innocent. We have been made a catspaw—how I cannot explain. You see, I am wholly frank with you. That is because I trust you, Ashton—and I don't trust many men, I can assure you."

This was getting interesting.

Whichelo, finding how much I knew, had unreservedly thrown off all pretence. I suppose he thought it his safest plan, as indeed it was. I had given him my word I would hold my peace if he dealt with me openly, and evidently he believed me.

From the morning-room we had strolled towards the back premises, and this conversation had taken place in the butler's pantry, quite a big room. The only door was immediately behind us. All the time we had been conversing—and we must now have talked for over an hour—the door had stood half-open. Now, happening, for some reason, to turn round, I noticed that it was shut.

"Hullo!" I exclaimed, starting up surprised. "Why, I thought that door was open!"

At once we dashed over to it. I turned the handle to the right and tugged at it; then to the left and again tugged. It had been locked from the outside—shut and locked so carefully, that we had not heard a sound.

I bent down to examine the lock.

The key was still in it—on the outside!

I drew back, and held my breath. What did it mean?

Chapter Twenty Seven.

In the Shadow.

Whichelo was at once practical.

He turned, and glanced quickly at the long window. It was securely barred, horizontally, as well as vertically. Then he pushed a table forward, clambered upon it, and exerting all his strength, endeavoured to wrench one, then another, of the bars from its socket.

A silly action. He could not stir one of them.

"Paulton has locked us in," he said, as he stood again beside me.

"Paulton!" I echoed.

"Yes—or Henderson. They and the Baroness—for whom I believe the police are seeking—are in hiding somewhere here. I thought it likely they would end by coming, as this is about the last place the police will be likely to search. They arrived yesterday, little knowing that I was in the vicinity. They're hiding in here. I happen to know this, though they don't know that I know it."

"But why can they have locked us in?"

"I can't say. Probably they're up to some of their old rascality. They are full of ingenuity, and defy the police at every turn. The first thing we have to do is to get out."

He looked about the long, narrow pantry. Soon his gaze fell upon a long-handled American fire-axe, suspended in a corner against the wall, beside a portable fire-extinguisher. He smiled, and crossed the room.

"When I lived abroad," he remarked, as he took down the axe and felt its balance, "I was rather a good tree-feller. Now, this I call a really beautiful axe."

Drawing himself to his full height as he spoke, he held the axe out at arm's length, admiring it.

"Its balance is perfect, and there's not an ounce of useless weight anywhere, either in the head, or in the stem. That is where American axes outclass our British axes entirely. Your axe of British manufacture is a clump of block steel stuck on the end of a heavy, clumsy stem. 'Sound British stuff,' it is, so the ironmonger will tell you. 'Last a lifetime. Last for ever.' And that is just what you don't want, Mr Ashton. In these days we don't need axes, or agricultural implements, or machinery, or anything else made to 'last for ever.' We want things made to last just long enough to give something better, time to be invented, and some improvements to be made, and no longer. That practice of the British nation of making things to 'last for ever,' has been the curse of our declining country for the past fifty years."

"But what do you want the axe for?" I asked, anxious to stop his sudden flow of oratory.

"What do I want it for?" he exclaimed. "Stand back, and I'll show you."

He stepped towards the door, and measured his distance from it with the axe-stem. Then, without removing his coat, or even rolling up his sleeves, he gripped the stem by its extreme end with both hands. With a "whizz" the axe described a complete circle over his head, then descended. The blade, striking the lock in the very middle, wrecked it completely. Another "whizz," another blow, and the lock fell in fragments on to the floor, with a metallic clatter. A third blow, and the door flew open.

I was about to go out into the passage, when Whichelo caught me by the shoulder and pulled me back.

"Scatter-brained Englishman!" he exclaimed, half in jest. "Doesn't it occur to you that Paulton may be, and probably is, waiting with a gun?"

I confess it had not occurred to me.

"Then how can we get out?" I asked quickly.

"Just wait," he answered, "and I'll show you."

At this moment we heard voices in the house, apparently in the large entrance-hall—men's gruff voices. Also there was a tramp of many footfalls. The murmur approached. A door opened and shut. Some of the men were coming along the passage in our direction.

They stopped abruptly, as they reached the pantry where we now stood. At once we saw they were policemen—plain-clothes men, in golf-caps and overcoats, yet by their cut, unmistakably policemen. They looked us up and down suspiciously. Then one of them spoke.

"Where are Paulton and his accomplices?" was the sharp inquiry.

"Somewhere in this house," Whichelo answered. "I haven't seen them yet."

"Not seen 'em! Then why are you here?"

Whichelo produced a card, and handed it to the speaker. Then he unfolded a letter he had withdrawn from his breast-pocket, and handed him that too. This letter was from Thorold, dated some days previously. It contained a request that Whichelo should go to Houghton and begin to make arrangements for his return there.

Satisfied with our bona fides, the police-officers looked inquiringly at the smashed lock.

"Well—and whose work is this?" one of the rural constables asked.

"Mine," Whichelo answered. "Some one, probably the men you want, locked us in. The only way to get out was to smash the lock. And so I smashed it. I advise you to be careful in your search. Most likely they are armed, and probably they will be desperate at finding themselves entrapped. How did you find out they were here, officer?"

"Two men and a woman, all answering the circulated description of Paulton, Henderson and the woman Coudron, were seen to alight at Oakham station from the last down express last night. They were followed. They hired a conveyance. Its driver was cross-questioned. And so we soon discovered their whereabouts."

Whichelo had, indeed, done well to warn the police-officers to exercise caution in their search—as it afterwards proved. For a quarter of an hour no trace could be found of the "wanted" men and woman, though the cellars, as well as all the rooms on the ground floor, on the first floor, and the second floor were searched.

In all, there were seven policemen. Whichelo and I accompanied them on their search, and I began to feel excited.

"What about the attics?" Whichelo suggested at last.

"I don't think they'll be there," the police-inspector answered. "I expect they've got off into the woods. Still, we may as well go up and see."

The attics, which constituted the servants' sleeping-rooms at Houghton, were very large and airy. A long, narrow corridor ran between the rows of rooms. Facing the end of this corridor was a door. This was the door of the largest room of all.

Some of the doors were locked—some not. Whichelo had keys belonging to all the rooms. The door at the end of the corridor the searchers approached last.

Whichelo eagerly tried two or three keys, but none of them fitted. He was forcing in a fourth key, when suddenly, with a deafening roar, an explosion took place within that room.

At the same instant something crashed through the upper panel of the door, leaving a torn ragged hole in the wood, and riddling the wall at the further end of the passage. Everybody sprang back with a cry. Then, to our amazement, we realised that nobody had been hit by the charge of shot, which had travelled straight along the passage. It seemed a miraculous escape.

The charge must have grazed Whichelo's shoulder-blade as he bent down to fit the key.

Scarce had we recovered from our fright, when the barrel of a gun was pushed through that hole. Those inside meant business. The barrel pointed swiftly to the right. There came a blinding flash, another deafening report. It turned quickly to the left, and a third shot echoed through the house. Wildly we had thrown ourselves flat upon the floor. The charges had swept over us, cutting great furrows in the wall on either side.

"Look out! It's a repeater!" I shouted, as I noticed the magazine beneath the barrel. "Keep back! Keep well away, all of you!"

The barrel swept from left to right, and right to left. It was resting on the smashed panel, and I guessed that whoever held it, had the butt pressed to his shoulder, and was endeavouring to discover our whereabouts before firing again. The fact that we might all be lying flat upon the ground, close to the door, apparently had not occurred to the man handling the gun.

Truly, that was a most exciting moment. Suddenly Whichelo moved. He was whispering into the ear of the constable crouching beside him. Swiftly the latter produced his truncheon, and Whichelo took it. Cautiously, noiselessly, he scrambled on all fours, then up to his feet. Now he stood upright, the truncheon firmly clenched in his right hand. Then, suddenly, grasping the protruding gun-barrel with his left hand, he dealt it a terrific blow close to the muzzle with the long, heavy, wooden truncheon.

And that single blow did it. The barrel, badly bent, was useless.

Quickly we all sprang to our feet and ran pell-mell down the passage. Though an ignominious retreat, it was the only move possible. Nor were we too soon. Hardly had we reached safety, round the corner of the passage, when another shot rang forth, and the wall facing the door was again riddled with pellets.

"They seem to have a battery," the inspector said, when we were once more in the hall. "We shall need to starve them out," he observed later. "There's no other alternative that I see. I've never seen such a thing as this before in all my years in the Rutland constabulary."

"Starve them!" I exclaimed. "And how long will that take? For aught we know, they may be well-provisioned."

"It's the only thing to do, sir," he repeated doggedly. "We can't smoke them out; and we can't very well burn them out; and I doubt if the law will let us shoot them, though they shoot at us."

"That may be so," Whichelo cut in quietly. "But I tell you this now—I'm going to take the law into my own hands."

The officer looked alarmed.

"You can't," the inspector exclaimed, as if unable to believe his ears. To your average police-officer the thought of a man's audacity to "take the law into his own hands," seems incredible. "You can't, sir," he repeated. "You can't, indeed!"

"You think not?" Whichelo said, coolly, gazing down upon them all from his great height. "Come along, Ashton," he called to me. "I'm going to teach a lesson to those vermin upstairs."

I followed him out to the back premises, and thence along a passage to the gun-room, the door of which stood open. As we entered, Whichelo uttered an exclamation.

And no wonder, for the room had been ransacked. The glass front of the gun-rack had been smashed, several shot-guns had been removed—I remembered there had always been three or four guns in this baize-covered rack, now there was only one—and about the floor were empty cartridge-boxes, their covers lying in splinters, as though the boxes had been hurriedly ripped open. The repeating-gun that had been fired at us was probably the Browning which Sir Charles used for duck-shooting, for this was among the missing weapons.

"They intend to hold a siege," Whichelo said, after a pause. "They've provided themselves with a stack of ammunition. This is going to be a big affair, Ashton, a much bigger affair than even we anticipated."

Carefully he took down the only gun left in the rack.

"This is of no use," he said, looking at it contemptuously. "It's a twenty-eight bore."

The outlook certainly was very black. True, there were nine of us. Had we been twenty, however, the situation would hardly have been better. For there, up in that attic, in a position commanding the full length of the corridor, were two desperate men, armed with guns, and provided with hundreds of rounds of ammunition, which, as we knew, they would not hesitate to use. The question which occurred to us, of course, was: how were they provisioned? Given food and drink to last a week, and who could say what damage they might do?

I went with Whichelo out into the Park. The woods were looking glorious. It was a perfect evening, too, soft and balmy, with that delightful smell of freshness peculiar to the English countryside and impossible, adequately, to describe in print.

We were perhaps ninety yards from the house, with our backs to it, as we strolled towards the copse. All at once a double shot rang out behind us on the still, evening air. At the same instant I felt sharp points of burning pain all over my back and legs. Whipping round, I saw a figure on the roof, outlined against the moonlit sky, just disappearing.

Whichelo too, had been badly peppered. Fortunately we wore thick country tweeds, and these had, to some extent, protected us.

Chapter Twenty Eight.

The Unknown To-morrow.

Take it from me. It is not pleasant to be wounded, even in a good cause.

To be shot in the back by a man standing upon a roof, with a scatter-gun, is not merely physically painful; it is, in addition, humiliating, because it also wounds one's *amour propre*.

At once I decided not to tell Vera what had happened. She was kind, sympathetic, and for many other things I loved her, but instinctively I knew that she would laugh if I told her the truth, and I was in no fit state then to be laughed at.

Indeed, merely to laugh gave me pain—a great deal of pain. It seemed to drive a lot of little sharp spikes into the holes made by the pellets.

Doctor Agnew—for I had returned to town that night, being extremely anxious to see Thorold again—to whom I exposed my lacerated back, made far too light of the matter, I thought—far too light of it. He said the pellets were "just under the skin"—I think he murmured something about "an abrasion of the cuticle," whatever that may mean—and that he would "pick them all out in half a jiffy." I hate doctors who talk slang, and I hinted that I thought an anaesthetic might be advisable.

"Anaesthetic!" he echoed, with a laugh. "Oh, come, Mr Ashton," Agnew added, "you must be joking. Yes—I see that you are joking."

I had not intended to "joke."

"Joking" had been the thought furthest from my mind when I suggested the anaesthetic. But, as he took it like that, and spoke in that tone, naturally I had to pretend I really had been joking.

Agnew picked out all the pellets, as he had said he would, "in half a jiffy," and I must admit that the pain of the "operation" was very slight. I should, in truth, have been a milksop had I insisted upon being made unconscious in order to avoid the "pain" of a few sharp pin-pricks.

Next day I went to see my love, and found her in tears.

Her father was, alas, worse, His temperature had risen. At the hospital they feared the worst. All the previous night he had been delirious. The sister had told her that he had "said the strangest things," while in that condition.

I tried to comfort her, but I fear my efforts had but little avail.

"Did they tell you what he said while he was delirious?" I asked quickly.

"They told me some of the things he said. He kept on, they declared, talking of some crime. He seemed to see things floating up before him, and to be trying to keep them from him. And he talked about gold, too, they said. He kept rambling on about gold—gold. The nurses didn't like it. One of them, I saw, had been really frightened by his wild talk."

This was serious. That a crime had been committed, in which Sir Charles Thorold had, in some way, been concerned, I had felt sure ever since that discovery in the house in Belgrave Street. It would be too dreadful if, while delirious, he should inadvertently make statements that might arouse grave suspicion.

Statements uttered by a man in delirium, could not, of course, be used as evidence in a Court of Law, but they might excite the curiosity of the hospital staff—they had, indeed, already done that—and though I am no believer in the foolish saying that women cannot keep a secret, I do know that a good many nurses are strangely addicted to gossip.

"We must, at any cost, stop his talking," Vera declared very earnestly. "What can we do, Dick? What do you suggest?"

What could I suggest? How deeply I felt for her. It would, of course, be possible to keep him quiet by administering drugs, to deaden the activity of his brain, but the doctors would never agree to such a proposal. Besides, such a suggestion would arouse their curiosity; it might make them wonder why we so earnestly wished to prevent the patient talking.

They might jump at all sorts of wrong conclusions, especially as they knew Sir Charles to be the man whose name had recently figured so prominently in the newspapers on two occasions.

No, the idea of drugging him, to keep his tongue quiet, must be at once abandoned.

We had just come to that conclusion, when somebody knocked. A page-boy entered with a telegram, which Vera opened.

"No answer," she said, and handed it to me.

The messenger retired. Scanning the telegram, I saw it ran as follows—

"Just heard terrible news. Also where you are. Returning at once. Engage rooms for me your hotel.—Mother."

The telegram had been handed in at Mentone.

Vera seemed a good deal relieved at the thought of seeing her mother again. At this I was not surprised, for, in a sense, she had felt herself responsible for Lady Thorold's evident ignorance of her husband's mishap and illness. She had felt all along, she told me, that she should have kept in touch with her mother.

"If my father dies, without my mother having heard of his illness, I shall never forgive myself," she had said to me once.

Lady Thorold arrived at the *Grand Hotel* next evening. She had travelled by the Mediterranean express without stopping, and had hardly slept at all. Nevertheless, she insisted upon going at once to the hospital, to see her husband.

He was a little better, the doctor told her. He had recovered consciousness for a short time that evening, and his brain seemed calmer. Several times, while conscious, he had asked why Lady Thorold did not come to him, and where she was. Her absence evidently disturbed him a good deal.

On leaving the hospital, I looked in at Faulkner's club. He was in the hall, talking to the porter, and just about to come out.

"Ah, my dear Dick," he exclaimed, "you're the very man I want to see. How is Sir Charles?"

"A very little better," I answered. "I have just come from the hospital. Lady Thorold is with him now."

"Good. By the way, have you seen the tape news just in?"

"What news?"

He led me across to the machine at the further end of the hall, picked up the tape, and held it out at arm's length. The startling words I read were as follows—

"The men whom the police are trying to arrest at Houghton Park to-day, shot three policemen dead, and seriously injured a fourth. A reinforcement of police has been summoned. Thousands of people have assembled in the Park, which surrounds the house, and hundreds are arriving hourly on foot, on bicycles, in carriages, and in cars."

While we stood there, the machine again ticked. This was the message that came up—

"Houghton Park. Later: A number of bags of gold coin, mostly French louis, have just been found at Houghton Park. They were discovered by the police, concealed between the rafters and the roof. There are said to be several thousand pounds worth of these coins."

So the mystery was slowly leaking out. I felt that everything must soon be known. How did those sacks of gold come to be hidden in the roof at

Houghton? Who had concealed them there? Could it be the same gold I had seen in the house in Belgrave Street? And if so, had Whichelo...

I felt bewildered. What chiefly occupied my thoughts was the news of those policemen. Poor fellows! How monstrous they should not have been allowed to fire upon the murderers.

Too furious to speak, I left the club with Faulkner, and together we walked along Piccadilly, towards Bond Street. As we sauntered past the Burlington, a pair of laughing, dark eyes met mine, and at once I recognised—Judith!

"*Ah, mon cher ami!*" she cried, revealing her white teeth as she extended her well-gloved hand. She was gorgeously and expensively dressed, in the height of Paris fashion, and I noticed that all who passed us by—men and women alike—stared hard at her.

"Did you come back with Lady Thorold?" I asked—why, I hardly knew—when we had talked for some moments.

"*Mais, oui*," she exclaimed. "We were together in Mentone, when I read in a newspaper about this dreadful affair. I had just heard from a friend here that Mademoiselle Vera was staying at the *Grand Hotel*, so I told Lady Thorold. She was *désolée* at the news about Sir Charles—*pauvre homme*—and said she must return at once to see him, and asked me if I would come with her. So I said, 'Oh, yes.' And here I am. Do you remember our evening together at the ball in Monte Carlo?" she ended, with a rippling, silvery laugh.

"Where are you staying?" Faulkner asked.

"I? At the *Piccadilly Hotel*. You must come to supper with me there. What night will you come?"

We made some excuse for not arranging definitely what night we would have supper with her, and I laughed as I thought of the two louis I had given the girl as a bribe to remove her mask, and of the sum I had afterwards paid her to take me to Vera. And now she was staying at the *Piccadilly Hotel*, and giving supper parties—the girl whom I had once believed to be Lady Thorold's maid!

How strangely wags the world to-day!

As we all three emerged into Burlington Gardens, boys came rushing past with the latest edition of an evening paper.

"*Ah, gran' Dieu!*" she cried, as she caught sight of the contents bills. For this was what we read on them—

HOUGHTON PARK.

SACKS OF GOLD DISCOVERED.

AMAZING STORY.

She snatched a paper from the nearest boy, but it contained only the news we had just read on the club tape.

Judith seemed more upset at the news of Sir Charles' condition, I thought, than about the "Houghton Siege," as the papers called it. She said she must go at once to Lady Thorold, and, hailing a passing taxi, left us.

As I looked at the pictures of Houghton Park, in that paper we had bought, I could not help wondering what the Rutland people must be saying.

Only a month or two ago, the sudden flight of the Thorolds from Houghton, and the events that had followed, had brought that exclusive county notoriety, which I knew it hated.

Then there had been the mystery of old Taylor's death in the house in Belgrave Street, and quite recently the mystery of the mummified remains, both of which events had again brought Rutland indirectly into the limelight of publicity, the Thorolds and myself being Rutland people.

Now, to cap everything, came this "Siege of Houghton Park," to which the newspapers, one and all, accorded the place of honour in their columns. It was the "story of the day." This final ignominy would give Rutland's smug respectability its deathblow. Never again, would its county families be able to rear their proud heads and look contemptuously down upon the families of other counties and mentally ejaculate—"We thank thee, O Lord, that we are not as these publicans." Henceforth, proud and exclusive Rutland would bear the brand of Cain, or what "the county" deemed just as bad—the brand of Public Notoriety. Yes, there is amazing snobbishness, even yet, in our rural districts. Yet there is also still some sterling British broad-mindedness—the old English gentleman, happily, still survives.

Faulkner had asked me to go to a theatre with him. He knew, he said, he could not ask Vera, with her father so ill, but Violet de Coudron would be there. He would try to get a fourth, as he had a box. There was no good in moping, he ended, sensibly enough.

I returned to King Street to dress, intending to telephone first, to the hospital, to inquire for Sir Charles. On the table, in my sitting-room, a telegram awaited me. Somehow I guessed it must be from Vera in her distress, and hurriedly tore it open—

"Father sinking fast," it ran, "and beseeching for you to come to him. Come at once. Most urgent—Vera."

I rang for my man. The telegram had been awaiting me about half-an-hour, he said.

Telling him to telephone to the hospital, to say I was on my way, and also to Faulkner, to tell him I couldn't go to the theatre, I hurried down the stairs, dashed out into the street, and hailed the first taxi I met.

Was the actual truth at last to be revealed?

Chapter Twenty Nine.

A Strange Truth is Told.

I went straight up to the side-ward in the hospital where Thorold lay, the hall-porter, in his glass-box, having nodded me within. At the door of the ward I met the sister, in her blue gown.

"I am so glad you have come, Mr Ashton!" she exclaimed. "He wants so much to see you, and I fear he has not long to live."

The dark-eyed woman, with the medal on her breast, seemed genuinely distressed. Thorold, for some reason, had always attracted women. I think it was his sympathetic nature that drew women to him.

I waited in the corridor. Suddenly Vera came out, a handkerchief saturated with antiseptic before her mouth, to avoid infection.

Her face was pale and drawn, her eyes red from weeping. On seeing me, she began to sob bitterly; then she buried her face in her hands.

I did my best to comfort her, though it was a hard task. At last she spoke—"Go in to him—go in to him now, dear," she exclaimed broken-heartedly. "He wants you alone—quite alone."

The invalid was quite conscious when I entered, a handkerchief similar to Vera's having been given me by a nurse. He was propped up with pillows into almost a sitting posture. The other bed in the side-ward was unoccupied, for it was being used for isolation. After what I had been told, I was surprised at his appearance, for he struck me as looking better than when I had last seen him. A faint smile of welcome flickered upon his lips as he recognised me. Then he grew serious.

Without speaking, he indicated a chair beside the bed. I drew it near, and seated myself.

"We are quite alone?" he whispered, looking slowly about the room. "Nobody is listening—eh? Nobody can hear us?"

"Nobody," I answered quickly. A lump rose in my throat. It was dreadful to see him like that. Yet, even then, I could hardly realise I was so soon to lose my valued and dearest friend, who had been such a striking figure in the hunting-field.

He put out his thin hand—oh, how his arm had shrunk in those few days!—and let it rest on mine. It felt damp and cold. It chilled me. The moisture of death seemed already to be upon it.

"Listen, Dick, my boy," he said very feebly. "I have much to tell you, and—and very little time to tell it in. But you are going to marry Vera, so it—so it's only right that you should know. Ah, yes, I can trust you," he said, guessing the words I had been about to utter. "I know—oh, yes, I know that what I say to *you* won't make any difference to our long friendship. But even if it should," he said, grimly, "it wouldn't matter—now we are so very soon to part."

I felt the wasted hand grip more firmly upon my wrist.

"I have known you for half your life, my boy," he said, after a pause, "and I'll tell you this. There is no man I know, whom I would sooner Vera married, than yourself. You have your faults, but—but you will be good to her, always good to her. Ah! I know you will, and that is as much as any woman should expect. And Gwen is glad, too, that you are going to marry Vera. But now, Dick, there is this thing I must tell you. I—I should not rest after death, if I died without your knowing."

Again he paused, and, in silent expectation, I waited for the old sportsman to speak.

"You have lately come to know," he said at last, "that there is to do with me, and with my family, a mystery of some kind. Part of my secret, kept so well for all these years, I believe you have recently discovered. The rest you don't know. Well—I'll tell it—to—you—now."

With an effort, he shifted his body into a more comfortable position. Then, after coughing violently, he went on—

"Dick, prepare yourself for a shock," he said, staring straight at me with his fevered eyes. "I have—I have been a forger, and—and worse—a murderer!"

I started. What he said seemed impossible. He must suddenly be raving again. I refused to believe either statement, and I frankly told him so.

"I am not surprised at your refusing to believe me," he said, calmly. "I don't look like a criminal, perhaps—least of all like a forger, or a murderer. Yet I am both. It all occurred years ago. Ah! it's a nightmare—a horrible dream, which has lived with me all my life since."

He paused, then continued.

"It happened in the house I had then just bought—my house in Belgrave Street. The governor had left me money, but I was ambitious—avaricious, if you like. I wanted more money—much more. And I wanted it at once. I could not brook delay. I had travelled a good deal, even then, and I was still a bachelor. During my wanderings, I had become acquainted with all sorts and conditions of people. In Mexico I had met Henry Whichelo, and on our way home to England on the same ship, we became very intimate. Another man on board, with whom I had also grown intimate, was Dan Paulton—or Dago, as his friends called him. A man of energy and dash, and of big ideas, he somehow fascinated and appealed to me. Well—he—he discovered my ambition to grow rich quickly and without trouble. He was a plausible and most convincing talker—he is that still, though less than he was—and by degrees he broke it to me that he was interested in, and in some way associated with, a group of 'continental financiers,' as he called them. Later, I discovered, when too late, that really they were bank-note forgers! He talked to me in such a way that gradually, against my will, and quite against my better nature, I became interested in the operations of these men. And, as he had thus ensnared me by his insidious talk, so, in the same way, he had ensnared our companion, Whichelo."

And he paused, because of his difficulty in breathing.

"It was about this time that I married. Within a year after my marriage, I found that blackguard Paulton was doing his best to steal Gwen from me," he went on, in a half-whisper. "He was talking her right round, I found, as he seemed able to talk anybody round. By this time, I had discovered him to be a far greater scoundrel than I had ever before suspected. Then came a revulsion in my feelings. I had come suddenly to hate him. My mind became set upon revenge. Already I had become actively interested in Paulton's continental schemes for making money, the forgery of French bank-notes, and by manufacturing coin. My fortune was already more than doubled. Alas! It was too late to draw back. Some of the base coin had actually been moulded and finished in my house in Belgrave Street. The rest was made abroad. The coins, perfectly made by an ingenious process, were nearly all French louis and ten-franc pieces, these being the coins most easy to circulate at the time. Paulton's plan for issuing the coin we made, was ingenious and most successful. It seemed impossible—of—of—discovery. And—"

Once again he was compelled to pause, drawing a long and difficult breath. Then he continued—

"It was the year before I met you that the tragedy occurred. Paulton, Whichelo, Henderson, and also a half-brother of Paulton's named Sutton, who was nearly always with him, and myself, were gathered in the room on the second floor, in my house in Belgrave Street, the room that was found recently with a hole cut in the floor. It was late at night, and the place was dimly lit. We worked in silence. The work we were engaged upon I need not trouble to explain to you—I expect you can guess it. My mind was in a whirl. I was thinking all the time of my wife, wondering how far her intrigue with Paulton had already gone. Then and there I would have assaulted Paulton, turned him out of the house, but I had so far compromised myself that I confess, I dare not. I could not do anything that might incur his enmity—he had the whip-hand of me completely—I, who had recently bought a knighthood, just as easily as I could have bought a new hat.

"Suddenly, some one knocked. Ah! How we all started! I was the first to spring to my feet. In a few moments all tools and implements we had been using, had been spirited away. They had disappeared into receptacles in the floor and in the walls, made specially for their concealment. Then I unlocked the door. Gwen entered. She had been dining out with friends, and had returned much earlier than she had expected. Her bedroom was far removed from the room in which we were at work, but she had noticed a faint light between a chink in the shutters, and so, on entering the house, she had come up to that room."

And he was seized by another fit of coughing, and pointed to a glass half-filled with liquid, which I placed to his lips.

"How surprised and startled she looked, at finding us all there, apparently reading newspapers and smoking!" he went on. "That was the first time she began to suspect—something. The glance she exchanged with Paulton, brought the fire of jealousy to my brain. I believe at that moment I went mad, for I loved her. I have a furious, a most awful temper. You have never, in all these years we have known each other, my boy, discovered that—and yet I say the truth. Yes—it—it got the better of me that night. Without an instant's forethought, I sprang across the room, crazed, beside myself with jealousy. I slammed the door and locked it. Then rushing at my wife—God forgive my having done it—I seized her by the arms, and flung her to the ground, charging her with infidelity, vilifying her most horribly, hurling blasphemy upon Paulton who, pale as death, glared at me. Then—ah, shall I ever forget that moment!" he cried, in agony of mind. "Then he sprang at me. I dodged him, and he slipped and fell. Instantly recovering himself, he made a second rush. This time his half-brother, Sutton, came at me, too, with a drawn knife. In my frenzy I picked up the nearest thing handy, with which to defend myself. It was a short iron bar, used for opening boxes, the only tool we had, in our haste, overlooked when hiding the implements. With one bound, Paulton was upon me, his half-brother just behind. As I aimed a terrific blow at him with the iron rod, he ducked. The blow meant for him struck Sutton just below the ear. The man collapsed in a heap upon the floor. He never spoke again. He died without a cry!"

The dying man moaned again in mental agony, and moved feverishly upon his pillow.

"Don't—don't tell me any more," I urged in distress, seeing how it upset him to recall what had happened.

"I must. By Heaven, I must!" he exclaimed hoarsely. "You must know everything before I die. I shall never rest unless you do. *Never!*"

He breathed with increasing difficulty, then went on—

"And—and seeing what had happened, Paulton, I truly believe, went mad," said the prostrate man. "It took Whichelo, and Henderson and myself, all our strength to hold him down. Gwen was on the sofa, in hysterics. What surprised me was that nobody in the street outside was attracted by the uproar. I suppose they couldn't hear it through the double windows. I won't go into further details of that awful night. I can't bear to think of them, even now. But from that night onward, Paulton had me in his power. It was Whichelo who suggested embalming Sutton's body and hiding it in the house. He would himself perform the embalming. He had embalmed bodies in Mexico, and understood the process."

He remained silent for some seconds.

"And so that was done," he continued. "Paulton and Henderson had left the house, the former satisfied at the thought that he could now use me as his cat's-paw—and by Heaven! he has done so! The coin we had in the house, some genuine, but most of it base, we hid away with the body between the ceiling and the floor. None knew our secret but my wife, Gwen—who almost revealed it during an attack of brain fever, which resulted from the shock she had received—Paulton, Henderson and myself. Vera was not old enough to know, but when she reached her seventeenth year, we decided to tell her the whole story, deeming it wiser, for various reasons, to do so. And now you understand."

"And during all the years I have known you," I said, "where has Paulton been? What became of Whichelo, and of Henderson? I met Whichelo for the first time in my life, just after you had left Houghton so mysteriously. Yet you say you have known him all these years."

"Whichelo joined his brother in Mexico City, and remained there for many years," he replied. "Paulton and Henderson continued their clever work of money-making, though mostly in Rome, and in Barcelona, where they had a number of accomplices. And I was bled—blackmailed by Paulton to the extent of nearly all my fortune—month after month, year after year. My wife, as you know, has her own fortune, and there were reasons why he could not touch that without incriminating himself, so for years I have had to live almost entirely on her means. Some years ago, Paulton and Henderson were both arrested in Paris on a charge of forgery of Russian bank-notes. They were tried, and sentenced to ten years' penal servitude. At the end of seven years, they were released. Paulton returned to England, and began once more to blackmail me. Worse, he had seen Vera, and at once told me he should marry her. If I refused my consent he would, he declared—"

The poor fellow who had once bought a knighthood, stopped, gasping for breath. I laid my hand upon his arm, as I thought to soothe him, but he pushed it off quite roughly.

"Some months ago he sent me an ultimatum. If I still refused to let my girl marry him, he—would call before the last day of—March—and—"

"Yes? Yes?" I exclaimed, unable now to restrain my curiosity.

"He declared he would disclose all he knew, take Vera from me by a plan that he explained, and that I saw I could not frustrate, and encompass the death of any persons to whom he thought I might have revealed the secret concerning him. Also he would tell the police the truth about the murder of his half-brother. He believed that you and I being such intimate friends, I had told you about him. Also he believed, for some reason, that my butler, James, knew something. He said he would kill you both. One of his accomplices was Judith, whom, a year ago, Gwen unsuspectingly engaged as maid. She, it seems, had kept Paulton posted in all that was happening in Houghton. I was driven to my wits' ends—entirely desperate—though—you—you never suspected it."

"But the photograph," I exclaimed, as I noticed a curious change suddenly come over him, "that photograph of Paulton—why was it at Houghton?"

"We always kept it there, that Vera might never fail to identify Paulton, should she ever meet him. When we told Vera, in her seventeenth year, all that had happened years ago, we showed her that portrait for the first time. It was my idea to set it in the morning-room recently, so that my poor girl might never forget what the man looked like who had sworn to take her from me."

"Could you not have removed the—that hidden body?" I exclaimed, anxious to get from him as many facts as possible, in the short time he had still to live. "What proof could he then have had—?"

"Don't—ah! don't!" he interrupted. "There were reasons—of—of course, had it been possible, I—a water-pipe had burst in my house—it had caused the body to stain the ceiling—and—also there were—" and his thin, bony fingers clutched at the air in frantic gesture.

His sentences were now disjointed, their meaning could not be followed. Now he was straining terribly his mouth gaped, his dry throat emitted a strange, rasping sound. I seized his wasted wrist. His pulse was almost still. Now his face was growing ashen, his eyes were staring into space—their intelligence was fading.

The nurse entered, and glanced at me significantly.

I sprang to my feet, and ran to the door.

"Vera! Vera! Lady Thorold!" I called. "Come—ah! come quickly, he is dying... *dying*!"

They rushed in from the corridor, where they had been awaiting me. In an access of despair, Lady Thorold threw herself upon her knees beside the bed, moaning aloud in a grief terrible to witness. My love stood beside her, gazing down upon her father—dazed—motionless. Grief had paralysed her senses.

Suddenly, his thin, white lips moved, but no words were audible. Quickly Vera bent over him. The shrunken lips moved again. He was murmuring. For an instant, his filmy eyes showed a gleam of intelligence once again.

"Dick—be good—to her—you—you will be good—*to her*!"

The voice was now, so faint, that I could barely catch his words. His dull gaze rested upon my eyes. I stooped down. My hand was upon his. Ah! How cold he was!

"Always," I said aloud, with an effort, a great lump rising in my throat. "I promise that—I promise I will do all possible to make Vera happy—always—*always*!"

By the expression, that for an instant came into his dull, filmy eyes, I saw that he had heard and understood. Slowly the eyelids closed. He was turning paler still. The light died from his face.

A few seconds later his countenance was ashen, and I knew that he had breathed his last.

Speechless, motionless, I still stood there.

My hand was still upon his, as it lay upon the coverlet, slowly stiffening. The only sound audible was the bitter wailing of his widow—and of Vera. I made no attempt to comfort them. Better, I knew, let the passion of their sorrow read! its flood-tide, and allow the fury of their misery to exhaust itself. Words of sympathy, at such a time, would only be a mockery.

Later, I would do all possible to help them to recover from the awful blow which had so suddenly fallen upon them.

Chapter Thirty.

Contains the End.

For a quarter of an hour we remained there in the presence of the dead.

The grey light in the side-ward faded into darkness. The electric light had not been switched on. The sobs and lamentations of Lady Thorold and her daughter, locked in each other's arms, began slowly to subside.

Gradually my thoughts drifted to the past, and all that had happened in those years I had known Thorold so intimately, and had loved him almost as a father. One thought afforded me most intense happiness. At last the time had come when I should be able to prove to Vera the intense love I bore her.

"Be good to her—you will be good to her—Dick—always," had been her father's dying request. Ah, how well I would obey my dear friend's last request! Never again should unhappiness of any kind cross his child's path, if I could prevent it. I would show her how, in my opinion, a husband should treat a wife.

My thoughts drifted to Houghton. What had happened there, I wondered. What was happening now?

Ah! What was happening! Had I known what was happening in those moments I should not, perhaps, have felt as restful as I did.

Next day the newspapers were full of it.

The "Siege," as they had termed it, had in truth become a real and desperate siege. All attempts to dislodge Paulton, Henderson, and the woman with them, had proved of no avail. Several policemen had since been severely wounded. This was due to the fact that the police, under the impression that the besieged men were armed only with shot-guns, had approached, as they believed with impunity, rather close to the house. All at once, a murderous fusillade had been opened upon them from a shuttered window—only by chance, indeed, had the result not proved again fatal. The wounds the police had received had been dreadful, far worse than bullet wounds, for the assailants had, by cutting the paper cases of the shot-cartridges round the middle with a knife, caused the charge of shot to travel like a bullet, which burst open when it struck.

"It was late in the afternoon," ran one newspaper account of the conclusion of the siege, "when a big body of police arrived from Oakham, armed with revolvers and rifles, to fire upon the besieged men, and in a few minutes the rattle of musketry rang out, the reports echoing and reverberating in the woods around Houghton Park, and among the distant hills. In return, came shots in quick succession, fired now from one window, then from another. The men hidden in the house seemed to have plenty of ammunition."

The reporter then indulged in half a column of descriptive writing. After that, he came again to the point—

"Finally, finding that all efforts to dislodge the besieged proved futile, and fearing they might, in their mad fury of revenge, set the house alight, the order was given to renew the attack. This was at once done. The combined fire played havoc upon the house for doors, windows, and shutters were quickly riddled, and even some of the chimney-pots were shattered. At last the return fire ceased entirely, and the order was given to rush the house. This was done, and only just in time. In one of the lower rooms straw, paper, wood shavings and other inflammable material had been piled up, and two paraffin-cans lay upon the floor, both being empty. Evidently it had been the intention of the besieged men to pour paraffin over the inflammable material, but they had found only empty cans. The material had been set on fire, but, not being well alight, was soon extinguished. At once a search was made for the besieged men—a risky undertaking, seeing that they might still be provided with ammunition and lying in concealment to open fire on the besieging party.

"It was in a shuttered room on the first floor that the bodies were at last found. The shutters had been riddled with rifle bullets. The two men and the woman were lying upon the floor, all three had been shot dead. Paulton had received no fewer than three bullet wounds."

There was much more, but I had read enough. I let the newspaper drop from my nerveless fingers.

Somehow, in spite of these terrible happenings, I felt happy—strangely happy.

At the moment, I had no time to analyse my feelings and discover a reason for the sense of restfulness that had come over me at last, after those weeks of hot, feverish excitement. Later, I knew it was the knowledge that all who could harm my well-beloved had mercifully been removed.

Lady Thorold, Whichelo and Vera were the only people living, besides myself, who knew the grim secret of Sir Charles' past life. No more would Lady Thorold, kind, gentle, sympathetic woman that she was, be haunted by the fear of blackmail, or terrorised by those human vultures who had so often threatened to reveal what had happened in the house in Belgrave Street in the dead of night years before. And, blessed thought, no more would my darling be harassed, bullied, or made to go almost in fear of her life.

And the gold—those bags of base coin found hidden so carefully at Houghton Hall, hidden there by Whichelo after their removal from Belgrave Street? And the mysterious body discovered in the house in Belgrave Street? Both had been pounced upon by the police.

But my only thought, my only care was of Vera—Vera, my beloved.

No doubt expert men from Scotland Yard were at that moment using all their intelligence, evolving endless abstruse theories, straining every nerve to pierce the mystery surrounding these remarkable discoveries.

I smiled maliciously, as these thoughts occurred to me, and I realised how fruitless all the well-meant endeavours must prove. For never, never now would any one find the true solution. The whole of the strange affair would be written down as a mystery.

Not until three months after poor Sir Charles had been laid to rest at Highgate, did our wedding take place, in Brompton Parish Church. And in the same week, at the same church, another wedding was solemnised. Frank Faulkner and Violet were married on the Tuesday, and I was present in the church beside Vera, who looked so sweet and smart in a pretty afternoon gown.

"Dick, dear, how happy they both are," she whispered, as Faulkner and his handsome bride passed down the aisle after the service, while the great organ pealed forth the strains of the old, yet ever new and never hackneyed, wedding march of Mendelssohn.

"And how perfectly lovely Violet looks," I answered.

Whichelo, who was beside us, and whose immense height had occasioned considerable comment among the invited guests, as well as some laughter amongst the crowd gathered together in the street, overhearing my remark, laughed aloud.

"A few more outbursts of unrestrained admiration of that kind," he growled, in his deep voice, "and I may hear from Thursday's prospective bride that my services as best man will not be needed!"

Well—what more is there to tell?

We were married two days later, at the same church as Faulkner and Violet—and spent a delightful honeymoon in Denmark and in Norway. Then we returned to dear old London, Lady Thorold having taken up her abode in a small house in Upper Brook Street.

Our most devoted friend to-day is Henry Whichelo—Harry, as he likes us both to call him. He knows everything of the past, yet no syllable of our secret will ever pass his lips. Not a week goes by but he dines at our table, full of his quiet humour, yet sometimes as we sit smoking together in the evening, the subject of those strange happenings—how fresh they still are in the memory of both of us—comes uppermost in our conversation.

"Ah, my dear old Dick," Harry said to me the other night, as we talked incidentally of the fire at Château d'Uzerche, "how I should have loved to see you sliding down that rope! Young Faulkner has often told me of your really wonderful sang-froid!"

My "sang-froid in moments of crisis" is now a standing joke against me! Vera, it was, who first started it, I believe. Well—I forgive her. I brought it on myself entirely, and must bear the consequences of my overweening conceit in the past!

A warm evening in August. The end of a stifling day.

As I sit writing the final lines of this strange narrative in my cosy little study in our new home—no, our home is not in tiny Rutland, but overlooking Hampstead Heath, a part of London that my wife loves—the crimson sun sinks slowly in the grey haze lying over the great city below. Vera is here with me, in her pale pink dinner-gown, and her fair hair brushes my cheek as she bends over me. Now her soft cheek is pressed to mine.

The blood-red afterglow burns and dies. The summer light is fading. The only sound is the whirr of a car going towards the Spaniards. The air outside is breathless, for the day has been terribly oppressive.

I raise my smiling face to her sweet countenance, and now, all at once, she stoops lower still, until on a sudden access of emotion, she passionately kisses my lips.

"Vera, my love!" I exclaim, looking up into her great blue eyes. "Why—why, what's the matter, my darling?"

Her eyes are brimming with tears. Her red lips move, but no words escape them. The corners of her mouth are twitching.

"My darling—my own darling, what is it?" I cry, rising to my feet, and folding my arms tenderly about her. Her head is upon my shoulder. She is weeping bitterly.

"Dick," she exclaims, hardly above a whisper. "Oh, Dick—my darling, my own darling boy, I have been sitting here thinking—dreaming of the past, of all we have been through—of those awful days and nights of anxiety and of dread terror. And now," the words came with a sob, "oh! I am so completely happy with you, my dearest—so absolutely happy. I can't describe it. I hardly know—"

The twilight deepens. I hold her closely in my arms, but I cannot trust myself to speak. Our hearts beat in unison.

Dusk grows into darkness. Still no word passes between us. We are too full of our own reflections, of our own thoughts, of our perfect happiness, now rid as we are for ever, of the grim shadow of evil once placed upon us by "The Mysterious Three."

The End.

Milton Keynes UK
Ingram Content Group UK Ltd.
UKHW012312040624
443649UK00007B/579